# NAZ & ROZ

## BETHANY-KRIS

Published by Bethany-Kris

www.bethanykris.com

ISBN 13: 978-1-988197-68-5

Cover Art © Bethany-Kris

Editor: Elizabeth Peters

For everyone who asked for Nazio.

# CONTENTS

# ONE

Music lit up the soul.

It certainly lit up Rosalynn's.

"Roz!"

Ivory keys of the piano felt the best under her fingertips when Rosalynn Puzza could shut out the rest the world, and focus on only the music she was making. Currently halfway through a ballad of her own creation for an upcoming audition, she had no intention on paying any attention to the voice calling her name from down the hall of her parents' home.

Didn't they know what she was doing?

"Roz, could you step away from the piano for a bit?" her father, Zeke, shouted. "We have to go!"

To nothing important.

Nothing that would make *music*.

Nothing like this.

Maybe that wasn't entirely true. The dinner party for her father's best friend's daughter and her fiancé *was* important to Zeke, and her mother, Katya. Roz remembered her father's best friend always being around from the time she was a baby. Or, as far back as her memories could go, anyway.

But that was the thing about Roz when she sat down at a piano and got to work. The rest of the world faded away, and nothing else mattered. She put her fingers against ivory, and became an extension of something *beautiful*.

Someone had put her in front of a piano when she was a toddler. She vividly remembered that moment standing on the bench in a poofy Sunday dress with matching yellow shoes that she'd *loved* because they looked like her ma's heels. The hands on her waist had kept her steady as she leaned over the keys, and smacked tiny palms into the ivory.

It made the *best* noise. There was something about the way the ivory felt under her hands, and the sounds the piano made when she kept hitting those keys that had clicked in her brain. It took very little time for her to realize if she did it a certain way, those noises became something else entirely.

No one had been able to keep her away from the piano since then. Oh, she got better, of course. She learned to make music instead of simply *noise*.

They called her a prodigy because she could hear notes, and mimic them perfectly by ear alone. They called her a genius with the piano because she could compose music in her mind, and translate it to the keys without having ever written it down. They said she was going to do amazing things because it was her *destiny*.

Roz just liked the music.

"Hey, can't you hear them calling for you?"

A hand landed on her wrist, and the second someone touched her while she was playing the piano, Roz's concentration was broken. She lost that focus because *someone* had to come into her space. Oh, sure, the ballad still played on in her mind even after the piano had stopped echoing her racing thoughts ... but *still*.

Glancing up with a scowl, Roz found her brother, Luca, standing next to the bench. He grinned in that way of his. A way that made her want to punch him right in the throat because it said he knew exactly what he had done.

It wouldn't be the first time she hit him. At only a year older than her seventeen, Luca was the typical big brother that liked to both overprotect, and annoy the *fuck* out of her. He took great pleasure in doing those things. She suspected it was because he was bored, needed to get laid, liked bothering her, or a mixture of all three things.

"What the *hell?*" Roz asked. "I was almost finished!"

She was running out of time to finish this original piece before her audition in Australia. She'd been enrolled in a private academy for the musically gifted from the age of eleven, but now she had a chance to be a part of an orchestra in Australia that would also allow her a solo spotlight in the company.

At seventeen, this was *unheard of* in her business.

She needed to be ready.

Luca arched a brow. "Dad's been calling for you for ten minutes, Roz. It's time to go to the engagement party for Cece."

Roz sighed, and glanced back at the piano. "But ..."

"It's still gonna be here."

This was not a battle she was going to win. While she loved the Donati family, because they had basically been a second family for her growing up, she doubted that she would find something over there to take her mind off the fact she left her music unfinished.

*Never leave a composition unfinished, Roz.*

Her mentor had repeated those exact words to her so many times that it was impossible to ignore. It didn't matter. Her brother wasn't leaving.

"*Fine*," Roz grumbled, standing from the bench. "I'm coming."

"Good." Luca clapped his hands once, and followed behind her. "Naz is home this time, too. First time you'll be seeing him in a while, right?"

Nazio "Naz" Donati.

Her father's godson.

Resident genius—*literally*.

Her brother's best friend.

Two years older than her.

The guy she had a crush on from the time she was *five*.

There were a lot of reasons Roz could list why she didn't care if Naz was home around the same time she was for the first time in years. Most importantly because he'd never seemed interested in being friends with her when he was closer to her brother.

But ... who knew?

"Yeah, maybe I'll say hi," Roz said.

Luca grinned as he slipped past her in the hallway. "You should."

The Nazio Donati that Roz remembered from the last time she'd actually had a conversation with him was a surly teenage boy who was more interested in fixing the laptop he'd broken in pieces on the kitchen table than explaining to her where she could find his mother. Roz remembered that moment in her life *vividly*.

She'd been fourteen.

He was sixteen.

Naz had no idea, and she'd been too embarrassed to explain, but she was looking for his mother that day because hers was not home. Katya had gone on a weekend trip to Vegas with a friend, and her father had been in the city for work. Likely for Naz's father.

Point was ... there was no woman nearby for Roz to have help her when she suddenly realized her first ever period had started. Of course, she'd been wearing a light-colored summer dress that ended up entirely fucking ruined.

She *did* change before making the trip through the trails that separated her parents' home from the Donati property, thankfully.

Eventually, Naz *had* listened long enough to her quiet, embarrassed voice whispering from the doorway that she was using to hide herself to say where his mother was. Catherine—as wonderful as she was—helped Roz, got her set up until her mom got home the next day, and it was like nothing had even happened.

Naz probably never knew the truth. He likely didn't even remember that passing day in his life. She couldn't forget it, though.

However, *that* brusque, distracted teenage boy with his black-rimmed glasses he wore as he tinkered with the broken electronic was not the same *man* standing across the room with an open beer in his hands.

Oh, sure, they looked the same ... that was, if the teenager had gained about sixty pounds of muscle, grew his hair a bit longer, hadn't shaved his face in a week, and could smile in a way that had Roz's stomach doing fucking flip-flops.

The house was full of people, which made it a hell of a lot easier for Roz to blend into the crowd. So was the way of mafia families. They were big, and whenever something important happened—like this engagement party—*everybody* had to show up just because.

Roz was using that to her advantage. She wasn't really a shy girl, but one look at Nazio from across the room as he greeted her brother, and she suddenly didn't know how to speak.

He was *just* a guy.

She'd dated guys.

Something in her mind said, *not a guy like that.*

A cute girl passed Nazio by and stared all the while. He didn't seem to notice her at all. He was too busy talking to Luca, and Roz was kind of mesmerized.

Like a dumb girl.

So what if his eyes were as dark as night. And who cared if his jaw looked like it had been chiseled from stone? Did it matter that he looked like he could probably bench press two-hundred pounds *easily*?

Apparently, her body cared.

It was strange—Roz had been so focused on being a world class pianist for the better part of her teenage years that things like boys and dating had been pushed to the side. Sure, she'd gone out occasionally with a guy, but that was it. It rarely went beyond one date, and she'd never found a guy who made her want to simply stare at him because of the way he looked while he fucking *talked*.

And to her brother, no less.

Luca told her to say hi.

*Ha.*

Roz wasn't quite sure she was up to that right now. If she opened her mouth and something stupid came out, she would *die*.

"There you are, Roz."

At the sound of Catherine—Naz's mom—Donati's voice, Roz spun around in her shoes. She didn't want someone to catch her staring. That would be embarrassing.

"How's it feel to be back in New York again?" Catherine asked, giving her a quick hug. "You know your mom and dad are so proud of you, right? They tell us everything."

Roz smiled. "I bet. And it's good to be back."

"I hear you have something huge coming up. An audition, right?"

She shrugged. "It's not that big of a deal."

"Not what I heard," Catherine said slyly.

"Okay, so it's kind of a big deal."

Catherine winked. "You're going to be amazing, Roz."

"Thanks."

The woman gave her another brilliant smile, and then someone behind Roz caught her attention. "Oh, there's Miggy. By the way, your father was looking for Luca. Could you let him know for me?"

Roz glanced in the direction she had last seen her brother with Naz. "Yeah, he's right over—"

*Not there now.*

"I'll find him," Roz said.

Catherine nodded. "Oh, and by the way …"

Roz glanced back at the woman. "Yeah?"

"You know, Nazio responds better when you *speak* to him, Roz … and not just stare at him. Conversation is what makes that young man's mind *go*. And once you make his mind start to go, the rest of him quickly follows. I blame it on the genius thing. His mind is the gateway to *everything*."

She blinked.

Apparently, her staring had not gone unnoticed.

Catherine grinned slyly. "Good luck. Have fun."

Well, then …

# TWO

Nazio Donati was a lot of things—patient in the face of bullshit was not one of them. And if one more person at this party thought that challenging his IQ was going to get them brownie points, he had news for them.

*Time for a breather, man.*

"Let's head outside," Naz said, already going in that direction. His companion followed behind without a complaint. Luca was good like that.

"Shit, I can't believe Cece is actually getting fucking *married*," Luca muttered.

Naz shot his best friend—and Zeke's only son—a look. "Believe it."

The nineteen-year-old Naz was only one year older than Luca, and sometimes, it didn't seem like the two had much in common from the outside looking in. Yet, they had been attached at the hip from the time Luca was born.

Naz had a pretty good memory—he blamed it on the fucking genius thing. He could remember still being in diapers, and looking over a little gray crib to see a baby dressed in a blue sleeper looking back at him.

Luca, that was.

"Lost my chance with her," Luca muttered.

Naz barked a laugh. "Fucker, you never had a chance with my sister."

"Asshole."

"Can't help that you're fucking delusional."

Luca punched Naz in the back of the shoulder as they weaved in and out of the people flooding the house for the pre-wedding party. Cece wasn't getting married for another month, but the celebration was in full force.

Any reason for an Italian to cook.

Or party …

They were all up for it.

Soon, Naz and Luca had pushed their way out onto the back porch where less people had gathered, and it wasn't as fucking suffocating. God knew he loved his family, but they could be a little too much when they all got together in the same house.

Usually, they threw big parties like this at one of the family's mansions where there was actual space between guests.

Cece wanted to have her party here at the Newport home. And Christ, their parents' Newport home wasn't even *small*. It was a three-level monster.

They just had a big ass family.

Like Juan, too, Cece's fiancé.

It was what it was.

"Here," Luca said.

He held out a freshly opened beer for Naz to take, and he was quick to down half of it in one go. He wasn't typically a big drinker, but New York was having some kind of terrible heat wave this summer, and his throat was dry from talking so much.

Another thing Italians loved.

*Talking.*

"So, what do you think?" Luca asked, leaning against the railing.

Naz shot his friend a cocked brow. "About what, man?"

"The whole Cece getting married thing."

"It's good," Naz said instantly.

Luca cocked a brow at that response. "Really, *good?*"

Naz chuckled, and tipped his beer up for another long swig. "You know, five or six years ago I might have had a different answer, but damn, that guy loves my sister. I don't have to worry about him treating her like shit … or having to bury his body in cement somewhere."

His friend laughed hard. "But you know if you still need to do that someday …"

"You will be the first fucker I call."

Luca's face split with a wide grin, and he held out his fist in offering. Naz answered it back with his own fist, and the two bumped.

Ride or die.

His brother from another mother.

"So, are you going to finally cut the fucking cord, and take the jump with me, or what?" Naz asked.

Luca sighed, and glared up at the sky like Naz was killing him. "You're never going to let that go, Naz."

"Well, it's a waste of time. You're going to be a made man like you're supposed to be. Just like I am, like my dad is, and like your dad is, too. That's what we're meant to be, Luca. You're just making the process longer by doing what you're doing now."

"So be it."

Naz shook his head, irritated.

"What the fuck are you doing in school, anyway? A lawyer, Luca, *really?* Come on."

"Says the man with a one-sixty IQ, Naz. Some of us aren't fucking blessed with a brain that just knows everything. Some of us had to wait to graduate at the right age, not early. Some of us didn't quit college because it was *boring*."

"I don't know everything. I didn't know everything from birth. I just happened to be really good at learning shit. And also, I didn't quit college because it was boring."

"Right," Luca drawled.

"I didn't. I quit because I had other shit to focus on, and getting my doctorate wasn't going to do anything for me in the long run when I was always going to be in the family business anyway."

"Whatever."

"A fucking lawyer, though. Jesus."

Luca rolled his eyes, and glanced away. "A *defense* lawyer, Naz. Who the hell else do you expect to save your ass when you need a good lawyer, huh?"

Naz stiffened, and hesitated on taking the next drink from his beer. "What?"

"You think I'm not going to be a made man?" Luca scoffed, saying, "I will, *eventually*."

"Mmhmm."

"I will, fucker. So it's going to take me a little longer than you, but that's okay. So I have to work a little harder for it between school, and Cosa Nostra, but that's fucking *fine*. You know why? Because there's a purpose to what I want to do—somebody's got to have our backs in ten, fifteen years. I don't mind being the fucker who does it, all right."

"You think that's what it's going to be?"

"What—you taking over for your dad?" Luca asked.

Naz shrugged. "I guess, yeah."

"Yeah, man, that's exactly how this is going to go down."

"All right."

Luca passed Naz a look. "All right? So what, you're going to get off my back about this school thing, now, or what?"

"Yeah, man. You do you."

Naz held out his bottle, and Luca clinked his own against the cold glass.

The two were quiet as they looked over the dark backyard. The noise level inside the house, and from the chatting people on the back deck was still quite loud. Naz didn't mind it so much like this. He was content—at peace.

Something his brain rarely found.

It was always chaos.

Always erratic.

"Hey, Luca, Dad is looking for you!"

Naz turned at the female voice calling for his best friend, and felt a million things hit him all at once at the sight of a dark-haired, ice-blue-eyed, tall beauty leaning out the backdoor. He knew who she was.

But he hadn't seen her since she was fourteen. She was a pianist, or something. Apparently, the girl was a prodigy. Kind of like him, but without the genius aspect. They put her in front of a piano at two, and there was no taking her away from it.

Or, that's how the story went.

She was in private schools, and privileged establishments meant to cater to her unique talent, and to grow her abilities. She usually came home in the summer, as far as Naz knew, and during the holidays, sometimes.

But a lot of the time, Naz was gone. Busy with work, or running guns. He didn't stay in one place for too long, and he didn't like crowds.

Maybe he saw her in passing, but his attention had been elsewhere.

Jesus Christ.

His attention was all on her right now.

*All on her.*

Back then, Rosalynn Puzza—Luca's now seventeen-year-old sister—had been just a girl. Too young to catch his eye, and too quiet to be fucking noticed. She had been stuck in that awkward stage of teenage life between just coming into her own, and still being stuck as a little girl.

She was not fourteen now.

She was very much a young woman now.

Naz blinked.

His mouth went dry.

*Christ.*

Gone was the gangly long-armed and -legged girl with a quiet, mouse-like demeanor. She took after her mother in her features—soft, pretty lines with high cheekbones, and wide eyes. Her pink lips were painted with a gloss that accentuated the way her mouth fell into a natural pout. She had to be five foot, ten inches without her heels on—she was wearing flats with the soft pink summer dress that fell loosely over her body.

"Yeah, Rosalynn, I'll be right in," Luca said.

Naz kept staring.

She stared right back.

Luca didn't miss it, either. "Shit—why, Naz?"

He didn't say anything.

Rosalynn smiled.

Oh, damn.

The girl was a special kind of beautiful when she smiled.

"Naz, right?" she asked.

Like she didn't know his name.

Like she didn't know who he was.

She *knew*.

He liked that she teased him that way, though.

Suddenly, his brain went quiet. All that chaotic shit that just never left him alone—all the things he learned and knew that constantly kept him awake unless he worked his body to the bone was silent.

He was not Naz, the genius. He wasn't Naz, the guy working to become a made man, and the gunrunner on the weekends.

His brain was struggling to remember how to talk to a fucking *girl*. His heart actually raced, and he was pretty sure his palms were sweaty.

It was crazy.

And amazing.

"Uh … Naz?" Luca asked, touching his beer bottle to the side of Naz's head. "You okay?"

Naz pushed his friend's hand away.

Rosalynn grinned wider. "It is, though, right? Naz?"

Finally, his incredibly *smart* brain decided to work.

Naz nodded. "Yeah, it's Naz."

"So hey," Rosalynn said, biting on her bottom lip, "maybe they're starting to dance a bit, if you want to come in and join me, *Naz*."

He didn't even have to think about it, or how he wanted to respond.

He *knew*.

Knew he finally found her.

Knew by the way his heart felt, and his soul was suddenly *alive*. Like there was some piece of him that had been waiting to find her, and now it finally had. And it was trying to crawl out of him, slipping around under his surface, and reaching out to her.

He *knew*.

His father used to say that's sometimes how it happened for men like them. All at once, and a lightning bolt that came out of fucking nowhere to strike them hard, and put them on their goddamn knees.

To remind them faith was real.

God was *good*.

Love was true.

"A dance?" she asked again.

"Yeah," Naz said. "I would love a dance with you, sweetheart."

# THREE

"Hey, wait up!"

Roz smiled even as heat climbed up her cheeks. She couldn't remember a time when she had seen Nazio speechless like he was outside, so she ... took a shot. It paid off *big time*. It wasn't like her to be so bold, but Catherine gave her the idea.

Naz slid in beside her as she headed down the hallway back to where the engagement party for his sister and her fiancé was in full swing. "Are you still at that school in England for music?"

"For now, yeah."

"It's been a—"

Luca pressed in between the two, and darted in front of them. Probably to go find their father, but who knew? Roz didn't miss the way her brother glanced over his shoulder to give the two a look, and then shook his head. Roz had never been the type to go after her brother's friends, and she was sure Luca was going a little crazy right now.

Oh, well.

She smiled back at him.

Luca darted around a corner, and out of sight. It left Roz alone with Naz in the back hallway.

"Anyway," Naz said, drawing in Roz's attention again. "It's been a while since I talked to you."

"Three years, actually."

"That's a shame. I missed out, huh?"

Roz's gaze darted up fast to find Naz staring at her the same way he'd done outside. Like he was seeing her for the first time, trying to take everything in at once, and didn't have the first clue what to do with it.

It was there—in his eyes—where she found a mix of softness, fire, and something else entirely. She didn't know what it was, but she *loved* that he was looking at her like that. That it was because of her.

Swallowing the nerves in her throat ... she refused to show them ... she asked, "Missed out on what?"

Naz's lips curved at the edges with a sexy smile. Easy, lax, and lazy all at the same time. Yet, it took his strong, handsome features and softened them just enough. He truly was a beautiful man, if that was the right way to describe it.

"Missed out on you, Rosalynn."

*Jesus.*

His words came out like a murmur. It felt like fingertips gliding over bare skin, and sent a shiver racing through her bloodstream. And the way he said her name? She thought it sounded even better than the music that played constantly in her mind.

*How?*

He only spoke two fucking sentences!

Those butterflies were back in her stomach. Beating faster with every second that passed. Making her feel a little too light on her feet, and taking her breath away. She only realized it then but the two of them had stopped in the hallway, and were staring at one another.

A few inches apart.

She wasn't even blinking.

What was air again?

"Missed out on me," she echoed.

Naz grinned in *that* way again. "Yeah."

"Maybe you should ..." *Now or never*, she thought. "... catch up, then."

At first, he said nothing. Simply kept staring at her like he was waiting for her to do something. Although, she didn't know what. Finally, he said, "That's definitely the plan if you want me to."

*Did she want him to?*

More than he could possibly know.

"How's the piano thing going?" he asked.

Roz couldn't help but laugh at that question. As random as it was, it was more the way he asked it than anything. "The piano *thing?*"

Naz shrugged one shoulder, and glanced away. "You got quiet; I got nervous. I blurted out the first thing to come to my mind."

Seems she had done it again.

Made him ... speechless.

"A mind like yours," she said softly, "and you don't know what to say?"

Naz cleared his throat, and chuckled. "Hey, this is new for me, too."

"I bet. The piano *thing* is pretty good, by the way."

"I hear you're fucking amazing, actually."

Her fingers twitched to reach out and touch those lips of his that seemed perpetually smirking or grinning in some way. Especially with the way he was looking at her right then. He called her amazing, and she wanted him to say it again.

"Funny," she said, "I hear the same thing about you."

Naz glanced upward. "Yeah, but I was just blessed with this genius thing. You ... you *learned* your craft."

She bet he had to learn a lot of things, too.

"Maybe I'll play for you sometime," Roz said.

"I would love that." Naz tipped his head to the side a bit, saying, "We were going to have a dance, yeah? You still up for that, or …?"

"Can you dance, or did you just say yes—"

"Don't be cute. I can dance."

This time, it was Roz's turn to grin. "Prove it, boy genius."

Naz smiled wickedly, and inched closer to Roz in the hallway. It wasn't like there was a whole lot of space between them now, anyway. She couldn't remember the last time she was this close to a guy, and felt *this* way about it. Like his cologne was soaking into her lungs, and her heart was about to pound right out of her chest.

It was *wonderful.*

"*Boy* genius," Naz murmured, nearly eye-level with her. She was a tall girl—it made things awkward sometimes. But with him, he had a couple of inches on her, and she liked that. *Loved* that she had to look up at him. "Let me know when you see a *boy*, Roz. Because I'm pretty sure this man is *far* from just a boy."

She swallowed hard.

He wasn't wrong.

"And if you want, I can even show you sometime," he added quieter.

*God.*

He was something else.

"A dance, then?" Naz asked.

He changed direction altogether but left her feeling oh, so crazy at the same time. He probably knew it, too.

"A dance," she agreed.

Roz was light on her feet when she danced—she blamed that on the four years she'd wasted in dance classes that ended up going nowhere because becoming a pianist had always come first. She could hear a beat, though, and she could move to it, too.

She was trying *really hard* to focus on dancing and less on the way Nazio's hands ghosted over her waist before grabbing tightly to her hips. She swore he only did that just so he could get her closer. Not that she minded.

She was, however, trying to maintain a little bit of dignity and space between them. It wasn't like there weren't a whole bunch of people watching them. Including *family*.

Her focus was entirely lost when the song blasting through the house changed to a slower tune altogether, and Naz spun her around with one hand. His arm curved tightly around her waist, so his hand could rest on her lower back while his other caught hers and wove their fingers together.

Roz laughed breathlessly when Naz winked. "I thought I said *a* dance, Naz."

"I wanted two. I'm not very good at denying myself things I want, Roz." Well, then …

She could hear the murmurings of the people around them. Despite the house being quite large, it was filled to capacity. Someone had decided the best bet would be just to move the furniture out of the living room so that they had room to dance, and mingle. The hallways were still full of people, too.

"Food's ready!" someone shouted.

Roz looked away from the man still staring at her to watch as people started to filter out of the living room into the conjoining dining room. "Aren't you hungry?"

"In a minute," Naz said.

His gaze caught hers again, and she swore it was like the floor tilted under her feet. "Why do you keep staring at me like that?"

Like the rest of the world didn't exist. Like this was the first time he was ever actually seeing her, but he intended to make it last.

"Catching up," he murmured vaguely.

"What does that mean?"

"It means … I don't know what it means," Naz admitted.

"Really?"

"My brain fails me today, apparently."

"That's a sad thing," Roz whispered.

Naz shook his head. "I don't think it is. I think it's pretty amazing, actually. My mind *never* stops, Roz. Even when I'm sleeping, my dreams are overwhelming because my brain just goes, and *goes*."

"And it's not right now?"

"It's going," he said, "just not like it should."

"Is that a bad thing or a good thing?"

"Right now, it's good." Naz tugged her a little closer, and her body tucked against his chest. Never once had he stopped moving them to the beat of the slow song echoing out of the speakers. Most of the room had filed out for food. A few people remained, but they weren't paying them any attention. "It's really good."

"Huh."

Naz quirked a brow, and his gaze drifted over her face slowly. "Can I take you home later? We could walk, or I can drive. Whatever."

The butterflies were back.

So was her racing heart.

He just … waited.

"You probably should," Roz said, "I might get lost."

Naz laughed. "You got it, sweetheart."

# FOUR

Naz didn't drive women home, let alone walk one. They were lucky if he called them a cab come morning, to be honest. It wasn't that he was purposely trying to be an asshole, but he was upfront about what he wanted or expected from a woman, too.

Usually something quick.

One night.

Even better if they were gone before morning.

That was it.

He didn't have time for more—his life didn't allow it. He was accustomed to handling the physical side of his life and needs as they came up, and moving onto the next task in his day. It was how his brain liked to micromanage *everything*.

Relationships and sex were the same thing.

Except ... he wanted nothing more than to walk Roz back to her parents' home simply because she said he could when he asked. He wanted five minutes with her where they weren't surrounded by everyone else watching.

Because *yeah*, they'd been watching.

His parents. Hers. Their siblings.

Fucking *everyone*.

Roz hadn't seemed to notice, and maybe that was a byproduct of the fact the girl was used to being on display, in a way. She'd have to be used to people staring at her considering how often she sat in front of a piano on stage, right?

Naz wasn't the same.

He noticed.

The genius thing made people pay attention to him, anyway. But that novelty quickly fucking wore off when people realized the only thing the genius thing did was make Naz smarter than them at the end of the day. It didn't make him particularly special—but he was just because he was him, and there was only one of him—or a goddamn superhero. He swore people thought just because he had a genius level IQ that some kind of magic was about to pop out of his ears from his brain.

That's not how it worked.

Nonetheless, he was very aware of the people around him at all times. It was partly because of the genius thing, and he wasn't fond of attention but also because of who he was. His last name and the legacy behind it meant Naz couldn't afford to *not* pay attention. The moment he decided to follow his father's footsteps in Cosa Nostra and as a gunrunner meant Naz no longer had the excuse of being distracted.

Even if he seemed like it.

So yeah, he noticed.

Naz was a lot of things.

Criminal.

Dangerous.

Quiet.

He was not, however, unaware.

And right now …

Roz looked over at him, and smiled.

He was also in love—how and why and all the rest, he didn't know. But it was the strange clenching of his chest every time he caught Roz's stare with his own; the way his heart *beat-beat-beat* like it was going to pound a hole right out of his chest; how he felt like if he took his sights off her for too long, she might fucking disappear.

Because he didn't know how this was real. How was something like falling in love with someone at first glance *real*?

But what else could it *be*?

Naz had been told his whole damn life that he was something amazing. That he was going to do great things, and not because he was a genius, but simply because he was *him*. Was this that great thing?

Was she his great moment?

Naz wasn't sure.

He sure as fuck wanted to find out.

Roz glanced over at him on the darkened trail, and though there was about six inches between the two of them as they walked, he had the greatest urge to grab her around the waist, and bring her closer. His heart and his mind just wanted her *closer*. And that was all before he got in to what his body wanted.

He ignored that bit.

Naz wasn't fucking this up because regardless of how smart he was, he was still a damn man at the end of the day. And men tended to fuck shit up just because they couldn't help it. Men thought with the smaller head between their legs, and not the one resting on their shoulders. He wasn't one of those. Or shit, he was going to try really hard not to be.

Not for her.

"Did you know our dads cut these trails when they first built the houses on adjacent properties?" she asked.

Naz's brow dipped. "I didn't know that."

He'd never asked, really.

Roz nodded, smiling. "Yeah, I guess when they were kids, they had trails connecting their homes. So, that's why they did it."

*Huh.*

Naz made a mental note to ask his father about that if for no other reason than he thought it was kind of ... interesting. And also because Roz told him. From the moment she shouted for her brother on that porch, Naz's mind had soaked up each and every single word that came out of her mouth. His brain was a sponge; it absorbed anything and everything it found *most* fascinating.

That's just how it worked.

And right now, everything in his world had shifted just like that. With nothing more than a girl he had known his whole life—but never really noticed until it was apparently the right time to—speaking. His brain flipped the fucking switch on him.

He no longer cared about running the numbers in his head for an upcoming gun run for his father. That was all easy going, anyway. Nothing for him to worry about even if he was *known* to constantly nitpick detail after detail until it was go time.

And he sure as hell didn't care about the current equation he'd been stuck on for a week as he tried to assume an infinite loop of time ran on the premise of an oval shape instead of the traditional figure-eight shape. After all, the usual figure-eight symbol implied at some point, time would have to intersect when it crossed over. There was no proof that—if infinite—time ever crossed over. And because he was such a fucking shit about things, Naz wanted nothing more than to just *see* if he could make the damn math work for it.

But that didn't matter.

*None of it mattered.*

None of it fucking mattered anymore because when Roz spoke, he *saw* her, his brain decided to shut the hell off in every other aspect ... and there she was.

*Here she was.*

She was suddenly the most fascinating thing in his life, and everything else could wait. His brain didn't want to factor in anything else at the moment. It was going to soak up every little thing she said or did because he *needed*—like he never needed anything else in his life before this very second—to know everything there was to know about her. He just had to.

"You're doing it again," Roz whispered.

Naz smirked. "What's that?"

"Looking at me like that again."

He still didn't know what that meant, though.

"Does it bother you?"

"Not even a little bit, Naz."

"Good to know."

Naz realized then that they weren't very far from the end of the trail that separated her family's property from his. *Shit.* That meant they weren't going to get to—

His thoughts silenced when he felt the light graze of Roz's fingertips gliding along the side of his hand. Before he could glance down to make sure she had done what he thought she just did, her hand slipped in with his, and her fingers wove tightly around his.

"That's better," Roz said. "Right?"

Naz smiled. "Getting there."

"How does it get better?"

"Let me show you."

Roz's eyes lit up with amusement. He thought all that bright blue staring at him looked far prettier when he sidestepped her to stop their walk. Naz moved in front of Roz without letting his grin falter for even a second. Her gaze never left his, and if anything, that smile of hers deepened into something *sexier*.

She knew exactly what he was going to do.

She was *waiting* for it.

Wanted it, even.

Keeping his one hand locked with hers, he used his other to slide around her waist, and tug her to him. Roz's teeth nipped along her fuller bottom lip as she stared up at him through thick, long lashes.

"Getting better yet?" she asked.

"You tell me."

"Almost, Naz."

He was about to make it a lot better for both of them. All it took was his head tilting down, and his lips sweeping over hers with a soft kiss. Gentle and slow, at first. Teasing with his tongue striking out to meet hers when her lips parted for him. Enough for him to get a taste of the sugar on her tongue from whatever sweet drink she'd had earlier, and the cherry flavored gloss painting her lips.

Just enough.

Just a tease before he was pulling away. He'd only wanted that taste just to *see* … he found kissing her could quickly be addictive if he wasn't careful. There was something about the way she watched him like that. All innocent in a blink, but absolutely capable of tempting his self-control in ways she probably didn't even know.

And then she grabbed him by his shirt with her one hand, and pulled him closer for a harder, deeper kiss.

Hell, if she wanted it …

Naz let her pull away when she wanted to that time. That gleam in Roz's eyes hadn't left, though.

"Now it's *way* better," she whispered.

Naz had to agree.

# FIVE

Roz kept sneaking peeks at Naz just to see as they walked the last bit of trail together. And yep, he was still staring at her. Someone else, and she might have gotten a little freaked out about the fact he wouldn't look away.

It was him, though. She didn't mind so much with him. Actually, she *really* wanted to keep his attention on only her.

"You know, if you're always looking at me," Roz teased, "you're not going to see what's coming on the trail."

Naz made a noise in the back of his throat. A *sexy* sound. It made Roz's stomach clench, and knees weak. His fingers squeezed gently around hers, and he smiled. "Not possible. I know these trails like the back of my hand."

Maybe he did. He and her brother had used them a hell of a lot more than she ever had as a kid.

"It's on you if you face plant right into the—"

Without warning, Naz let go of her hand, circled a strong arm around her waist, and lifted her right from the ground. Two steps later, he put her back down like he hadn't done anything in the first place. Roz peeked over her shoulder to find the bent root of some tree sticking out a good four inches from the ground. She hadn't even seen that and easily would have tripped over it. Maybe scuffed up her hands a bit when she tried to break her fall. *That* wouldn't have been good at all.

Not for playing the piano, anyhow.

"We found that root when Luca wrecked his dirt bike, and cracked his tooth in half," Naz said.

Roz's brow knotted together. "Wasn't that when he was twelve?"

"I was thirteen."

"He told Ma he tripped running back from the park. And I remember her calling *your* parents just to find out if you'd been with him or not when it happened."

"And I backed him up, yeah." Naz smirked. "Maybe we weren't wearing helmets like we'd been told to do. *But* ... you didn't hear that from me."

*Huh.*

"Is that a common thing for you two?"

Naz arched a brow, and glanced over at her. "What's that?"

"Lying for one another."

"I wouldn't call it *lying*," he murmured, his hand tightening around hers again. "More like ... watching each other's backs. That's what we were taught to do, after all. If they didn't want us looking out for one another, then they wouldn't have stuck us together the first moment they could."

That was true.

Roz couldn't deny it.

For as long as she could remember, her brother had always tagged along with Naz. Where one went, the other was quickly followed. Their parents had always been quick to encourage the two boys' friendship, too.

Rarely had they been told no.

"I bet you two have done that quite a bit, haven't you?" she asked. "Lie—oh, I mean, *watch each other's backs*."

She didn't even try to hide the teasing lilt to her tone. Naz didn't miss it if the way the sly gleam lit up his gaze was any indication.

Naz grinned. "It's very possible."

"Care to tell me some?"

"Maybe someday."

His tone did not match his statement. He sounded like, no, he didn't plan on telling her very much in that regard. *Boys.*

Roz rolled her eyes, and laughed. "You're not going to tell me anything, are you?"

"Probably not."

"Why?"

Naz shrugged. "Honestly, it's probably better you *don't* know some of the shit we've pulled. I can't say all of it is as funny or innocent as the dirt bike story, Roz."

Well ...

"I'd still like to hear it."

Naz made another one of those noises. "Maybe someday."

She thought he sounded more believable that time. But who knew?

Roz took the front steps of the porch slowly, and only glanced back at Naz when she pulled the keys to the house out of her pocket. "Do you ... want to come in?"

He hadn't climbed the stairs with her. He just stayed there leaning against the railing of the stairs as she started to unlock the door.

"Do I want to and should I are two entirely different questions," Naz murmured.

"What does that mean, exactly?"

Although, she wasn't a stupid girl. And she was pretty damn sure she knew exactly what it meant.

Naz inched up one step slowly. A bit closer to her, but as her heart was screaming and pounding in her chest, he still wasn't nearly close enough. She didn't know what to do with these strange feelings this man invoked. Not the odd ache between her thighs, or the shortness of breath she had every time he looked at her like he was right now.

"It means," Naz said, "that I absolutely want to go inside with you. More than you know, Roz. But I *shouldn't* because I know better. Because it's not the right thing to do tonight, even if I am a selfish little fuck."

She grinned.

He came a little closer.

"Then, why are you still climbing the stairs, Naz?"

"For this."

He darted forward from the last step, and closed the distance between them. His hands found her face, and he tipped her head back a second before his mouth crashed down on hers. The sweet kiss from earlier was entirely gone as his tongue struck hard against the seam of her lips.

*Demanding*, she thought. He was demanding she open for him, and let him taste her again. She liked that, and didn't mind obliging. There was something *wicked* about the way he kissed her. How it made that ache between her thighs turn into a low flame that reached deep inside her body. Her skin *hummed*. He nipped her bottom lip gently, and then kissed her again.

By the time Naz finally pulled away—although he never once took his hands off her face or moved his gaze even a fraction of a millimeter from hers—Roz was trembling and she didn't think she could talk.

"Had to do that one more time," Naz said lowly.

There was something about the way he talked after he had his mouth on hers—husky, and dark. A lovely tone that had her muscles clenching all over and unsure of what to do. But oh, she liked it. She most certainly liked it.

Too much, maybe.

"You should do that more often, then," Roz said.

Naz grinned in that way of his. "I will."

"But you're not coming in."

"Not tonight," he returned.

"Okay."

"I would like to take you out, though."

Roz's teeth bit down on her bottom lip as she mumbled, "Like a *date*?"

"Exactly that, Roz."

"When?"

"As soon as you want to go," he said.

Roz let out a slow breath. "You better figure something out quickly, then."

He let out another one of those hard laughs, and finally let her go. Not that Roz liked that all too much. She would much rather have his hands back on her. She liked it way better that way. When he was touching her, everything else seemed to disappear. It already felt like the whole goddamn world was constantly watching her anyway. If he could make that disappear, she didn't mind at all.

"Where's your phone?" Naz asked.

Roz pulled the device out of her pocket, and handed it over without question after unlocking it. Naz plugged in digits, and handed it back over with a wink.

"Just in case you … get bored," he said, "you know who to call."

She smiled down at her phone. "And that date?"

"That's definitely happening, too."

*Good.*

# SIX

Naz wasn't exactly fucking surprised to find Luca leaning against the entrance door of his apartment complex.

Luca cocked a brow at the sight of him, and flicked the ash from his cigarette over the railing. "Took you long enough, didn't it?"

Naz laughed under his breath. "Seriously?"

His friend kept staring at him … like he was waiting for something. "Yeah, Naz."

It'd taken him a good hour and a half to get back to the city after saying goodbye to his parents—who *both* looked like they had questions about where he'd gone with Roz, but also chose not to ask. At least, not yet. His parents tended to mind their own business where he was concerned, and he liked that just fine. That way, when they did ask something, he found it easier to tell them.

But he certainly hadn't been gone long enough that Luca should be acting like a cocksucker. Then again, Naz *had* kind of taken his best friend's sister away from the party without much of a word.

"I walked her home, asshole," Naz said, tugging the apartment keys from his pocket. Luca slipped in behind him as he unlocked the front door to the apartment complex. He preferred living in the city when it came to work. He was always running for his father or Zeke when it came to the Donati Cosa Nostra, and that business never stopped. It was almost always in the city, too.

Luca cleared his throat as the two of them stepped into the main entrance. Naz shot his friend another look, this time, one that silently said, *Get it out, or shut the fuck up.*

"Just so you know, Dad has cameras all over that property," Luca muttered.

Ah, yeah.

"Forgot about that," Naz murmured.

He shouldn't have forgotten about it, though, to be fair. Men like Zeke—and even his own father—tended to keep a close eye on their properties because the very nature of their business meant the first thing an enemy attacked was wherever a man called *home*. Plus, made men were just paranoid in general. That couldn't be helped.

"Well, damn," Naz added under his breath. "Let's hope he doesn't watch very much, I guess."

Luca's fist slammed into the back of Naz's shoulder with a sharp *snap*. Naz jerked forward from the hard punch with a choked laugh. Because shit yeah, while it was funny, it still fucking hurt, too.

"*Fucker*," Naz said, a little breathless.

"*You're* the fucker. Who shouldn't be messing around with my *sister*!"

*Really?*

That's what they were going to do?

Naz didn't think so. "Shut up until we get into my place. I don't feel like getting another noise violation fine because you wanna be a shithead, Luca."

His friend followed behind him, and thankfully, mostly stayed quiet. Except for the occasional grumble under his breath, that was. Naz could practically feel Luca's glare burning into his back, though.

Luckily for Luca, his friend didn't have to wait very long before he was able to open his mouth, and go off again. Naz lived on the bottom floor—his father *hated* that for a number of reasons—and close to the end of the hallway.

The moment the apartment door closed behind them, Luca started bitching. Naz basically tuned his friend out as he shrugged off his leather jacket, and pulled the beanie from his head. He didn't need to actually listen to Luca to know what the guy was saying, so, what was the fucking point in wasting time with that?

Naz pulled the pair of black-rimmed reading glasses out of the inner pocket of his jacket before hanging it up on a rack. He only really needed those damn glasses when he was going to read in bed, or he planned to stare at a computer screen for longer than a couple of hours at a time. Less strain on his eyes, or some goddamn bullshit. But who knew where he was going to be from today to the next—his situation was always changing—so he kept them on him just in case.

Luca was still barking off behind Naz as he headed deeper into his Brooklyn apartment. The place wasn't much to look at, as far as that went. Hardwood floors with a few too many scuffs, and standard white paint on every wall and ceiling. Even the light fixtures weren't anything interesting, really. Two decently sized bedrooms—which wasn't all that easy to find in New York—the standard living room, kitchen, and bathroom.

It certainly wasn't the *Marcello mansion*, from his mother's side of the family. Or even the large Donati home from his father's side of the family. The shitty little apartment wouldn't hold a flame to his parents' home which had been designed and decorated by the best of the very best interior designers in New York.

But it was *his* place. And it did the job considering how often Naz had to come and go from the apartment. He never actually got to enjoy his place for very long before he was up to do someone else's business for Cosa Nostra, or he was taking a trip out of the country for a month on the next gun run for his father.

He did manage to get the extra bedroom set up into his home gym. He desperately needed that. And he was able to get some shit up on the walls to decorate. The art he liked, and things he'd collected over the years. A hand drawing of a brain stem. A conceptual painted piece of what someone believed DNA to look like. And things that had nothing to do with that kind of shit, too.

So yeah, the place wasn't much … he could absolutely afford the penthouse suite in the middle of Manhattan if he wanted it, but this was perfectly fine.

For now.

There was even a little set of glass French doors that led out to a small, fenced private section where Naz could chill outside.

*That* was the part his father hated.

Someone could break in.

Someone could get at Naz.

*Right.*

Fuckers could *try*.

Naz invited anyone who thought they were quick enough and smart enough to attack him to make the attempt, and see how that fucking worked out for them. He didn't come from regular men—he didn't think or act like one, either.

Luca was still going on even as Naz pulled a bottle of water from the fridge, cracked it open, and took a long swig of the cool liquid. He hadn't been listening to anything his friend was saying because none of it mattered. Who gave a shit if Luca was stuck in his feelings about Naz taking an interest in Roz?

It didn't make a difference. Frankly, Luca and Naz had been friends long enough that Luca should already know that Naz was going to do whatever the fuck he wanted to do. Nothing anyone said ever made a difference to what Naz wanted. And right now, he *really* wanted Roz.

It was only a passing comment from Luca that finally made Naz start listening a little closer to his friend's rant.

"And she's not even supposed to be dating right now, for fuck's sake," Luca bitched, grabbing his own bottle from the fridge. "*And*, because there's more, I know how you are with females, Naz. You jump from one to the next, and you don't stay with any for very goddamn long. My sister isn't like some chick you pick up at the club—you can't be messing with her like those women."

"Go back a second," Naz said.

Luca shot him a look. "What? Are you going to fucking deny you don't even actually *date* when it comes to women, you just bust a nut, and move the hell on? Try to deny it."

Nah, he wasn't going to deny that at all.

"First of all," Naz said, giving his friend a raised brow, "you know my life is chaotic, and busy. I don't have time to be giving a shit about making sure the same woman wakes up in my bed every day, or that a woman even wakes up in my bed, for that matter. I don't bring them here. Second, I don't fill those females' heads full of bullshit, either. They know *exactly* what they're getting when it comes to me. I don't pretend it's something else, Luca. So, fuck off with the judgment, huh? Let's not act like you're a fucking saint, asshole."

"I didn't say I was, but there you go." Luca waved at him with a dismissive gesture. "You said it, man. *That* is what you like to do—you're not looking for more. Roz can't be like that for you. Don't use my sister, got it?"

"Just …" Naz shook his head. "Fucking *relax*, Luca. I like her. It's not about the rest. I walked her home, and kissed her goodnight. By far the *most* innocent shit I have ever done with a girl, all right? Chill the hell out."

Luca cleared his throat, and eyed Naz in that way again that made him feel like a bug under a microscope. Too many people in his life did that shit. Like they didn't know what to make of him, and they were trying to figure him out.

"What?" Naz snapped.

Luca shrugged. "Nothing."

"Really, *nothing*? Because you just ranted and bitched for ten minutes, and now it's *nothing*, Luca?"

"Swear you're not fucking around with her just to fuck around?"

Naz sighed, and glanced up at the ceiling. He had a good mind to tell his friend to mind his fucking business like he would any other time, but Naz understood why Luca was being a sensitive little ass right then. It wasn't *any other* girl. It was his sister.

Naz wasn't fucking with Roz, though.

Not like that, anyway.

"Swear it," Naz said, "it's not like that."

"All right," his friend murmured.

"Now go back—why the fuck can't she *date*?"

"Because her whole life is basically controlled and dictated by furthering herself as a pianist, Naz?"

He simply stared at his friend and waited for Luca to explain more. Because that shit right there made no sense. He didn't see why Roz couldn't further her career, but *also* have a goddamn life. He did exactly that as a man trying to get his button for the mafia, running guns on the weekend, and a genius that constantly needed to feed his need for knowledge.

Surely, letting Roz have a bit of fun—she wasn't even eighteen yet—wasn't going to do anything bad for her career or focus.

Or would it?

Naz had no idea.

Luca made a noise in the back of his throat. "Her mentor sent her here for a while to relax and prep for the upcoming audition in Australia. He's an asshole, but he's the best one to teach her. Or, that's what everybody else says."

Naz's gaze narrowed. "That plays in to the no dating thing how—"

"His rules. That's one of them."

He tipped the water bottle up as the phone in his pocket buzzed, and took another sip of water. Pulling the phone out, Naz grinned at the name lighting up his screen.

*Roz.*

She decided to text him, apparently. Nothing particularly earth-shattering or whatever, but still. A text was a text, and the night wasn't even over yet.

*Hey,* it read.

"Sucks for her mentor, then," Naz said. "Because I think that rule is shot to hell after tonight."

Luca just laughed, and shook his head. "You're so good at stirring shit."

He really was.

That's not what this was, though.

# SEVEN

*Bang. Bang. Bang.*

"Get up, Roz, your laptop keeps chiming. It's probably—"

"Fucking *Kyle*," Roz grumbled under her breath. Then, she added louder, "Ignore it."

"Roz, he's not going to stop."

Oh, she knew that. But he *might*. And she was totally willing to take that chance. All she needed to do was ignore him long enough, and maybe he would stop trying to get ahold of her this early. He'd already called and texted her phone until the inbox was full. She'd not answered any of those this morning, either.

A call to her laptop could work the same damn way.

She yanked the blanket higher over her head, and rolled over for extra good measure. She wanted to stay in bed, close her eyes, and go back to dreamland where her mind was filled with thoughts of a dark-haired, brown-eyed man. *Naz* was a far better thing to think about first thing in the morning instead of her fucking mentor who just wanted to drive her up the wall.

He'd been the one to send her here, after all. *He* was the one who thought spending a couple of months with her parents and away from the suffocating restraints of the school would do her some good before graduation and the big audition.

*Technically*, Roz already had her graduation in the bag. All her credits were in—her finals for the most important classes were written. The last ones she had to finish when she went back were add-ons, and not even important in the grand scheme of things. She took them because she needed something to fill the time between two o'clock in the afternoon, and four when she went in for three hours of practice.

"Roz, it's chiming again, so—"

"Ugh, I'm *coming*," she muttered, throwing off the blankets. Behind the door, she could hear her mother laughing quietly.

Kyle wasn't going to stop until Roz got up, answered his call, and handled whatever he wanted for the day. She was supposed to be focusing on herself, on composing and practicing. Anything but *him, the school, and everything there.* This trip home was intended to clear her head, and get her in the right headspace for the audition.

Except that couldn't happen at all because Kyle wouldn't quit calling every single day. Usually, that's exactly how he started her morning was by calling her. Asking *questions.* Too many questions, maybe. How long had she practiced the day before? Had she finished that last stanza? Corrected the intro like he wanted? Had she been able to pick up the pace near the middle of the composition, and had it maintained its strength?

*All the goddamn questions.*

Always about music, too.

Like Roz didn't know what she was doing, or something. She damn well did know what she was doing, but it went even beyond that. She needed to be confident in this piece she planned on playing for the audition in Australia. How could she do that when even her mentor wouldn't back the hell off long enough to let her enjoy what she was creating?

*Just deal with him,* her mind said, *and get back to your happy place.*

Yes, her happy place.

In bed.

Dreaming about Nazio.

Roz grabbed her blinking phone—Kyle's name was right on the front screen showing the last texts and calls she'd missed—before she padded to the door. Swinging it open, she found her mother had already disappeared down the hallway.

She'd set her laptop up in the living room the night before to let it charge, and *hope* that if Kyle did call, her parents would just ignore it. She'd hoped for too much.

Rox ignored the murmurings coming from the kitchen as she headed inside the living room. Plopping down on the couch, she grabbed the laptop with one hand, and raked her fingers through her loose hair with the other to push the wild waves out of her face. She didn't even get the chance to call Kyle back through Skype before his next call was already ringing through.

*Jesus.*

That man needed to relax.

Roz hit the answer button, and forced something resembling a smile onto her face. The second her blond, blue-eyed mentor that was edging closer to forty every day appeared on the screen, she said, "Morning."

*Politely,* too.

How Roz managed that, she would never know.

"There you are," Kyle said, sighing heavily. "You had me worried."

Yeah, she was sure. But not really.

"You can see me. I'm fine."

"Good thing. Wouldn't want the next *lead* pianist for the Cordana Company to stop before she really got started, now would we?"

Kyle Mathus had come into the school Roz attended with the intention to mentor a cello prodigy. All she remembered was being in her favorite music room, and playing a piece she had finished after working on it for over a year. After looking up from the piano, there Kyle stood on the other side of it.

He'd been a pianist for one of the world's largest and most successful companies. He'd played with orchestras all over the world. And then an accident irreparably damaged the tendons and nerves on one side of his left hand. He chose to mentor younger prodigies after that incident.

Roz was his third.

All his other students had gone on to be amazing things. They did amazing things. And his life—on paper—as a pianist was everything she thought she wanted to be. She was also seventeen—almost eighteen—and couldn't remember a time these last few years where she didn't look at this man's face at least once a day.

She couldn't just be a young woman when she was also this man's student. She had to be all the things he told her to be instead.

"Did you shut your phone off, or what?" Kyle asked, dragging Roz back to the conversation.

"Did it keep ringing, or just go right to inbox?"

The man's brow dipped. "What?"

"What did my phone do when you called—ring and ring, or go to inbox right away?"

"Rang and rang," he said.

"Then, I didn't shut it off."

Kyle frowned. "So, I am to believe that means you were purposely ignoring me."

"Or trying to *sleep*."

"You don't need more sleep, Roz. Not when you're going to bed at nine every night, and waking up at eight."

Yes, because even her sleep schedule was determined by this man when something as important as the Australia audition was coming up. She was pretty sure if she suggested he take over prepping meal plans for her, he would go ahead with that, too.

It was *crazy*.

"You need to prepare," Kyle continued on, repeating the same shit he said each time they talked. It wasn't new shit, and Roz was already starting to daze before he even really got going with his tirade. "As much and as often as you can manage. With and without people watching. At different times each day. Did you record your final session of the day yesterday for me to hear it?"

*Shit.*

She had meant to—it was the one thing she did like to do for Kyle. Even if she didn't take all of his suggestions when it came to changing her piece for the audition, he had a good ear. Better than good, really. He could *hear* her missteps when even she couldn't pick them out. He could hear— even through a recording—where she might have hit the keys a little harder than was necessary. He did make her music better.

He *did*.

And that was the whole reason why, despite a lot of the nonsense, Roz was grateful for Kyle. He was making her a better pianist.

She wanted to be the best.

He was giving her that.

"Can I assume by your face that your answer on the recording is a no?" Kyle asked.

Roz gave the man on the screen an apologetic smile. "I had a thing yesterday that I forgot about. A family friend had an engagement party. I *was* working on the piece, and meant to record the final run through … but someone interrupted, and I forgot by the time I got back."

Kyle raised a brow. "Are they?"

"Pardon?"

"Interrupting you often. *Distracting* you, Rosalynn. You know why you're there. This is supposed to be—"

"My parents are great," she interjected fast, wanting to put that to bed before Kyle got that on his mind. The man had a habit of running with nonsense when he got something in his head that he believed to be true. "I just forgot I had other obligations yesterday, and didn't get home until late."

Actually, she had gotten home at a fairly decent time. Sure, the sky had been dark, but if she had cared enough to sit down at the piano once she was home, she absolutely could have recorded her doing a run through of her piece for Kyle. But her mind had been on something else entirely.

*Naz.*

Certainly not in the right place to play.

At least … not with the piano.

Kyle sighed in that way of his again. "Do be sure to record it today. *Do not* let anyone take your focus away right now. Live and—"

"Breathe the music," she finished for him. "I know."

The buzzing of her phone in her lap made her glance down to see who the caller was. The name flashing on the screen caused Kyle's voice coming through the laptop to be nothing more than a buzzing noise in the back of her mind.

*Better things are here.*

Nazio.

Roz grabbed the phone, and glanced up at the screen. "Talk later, okay?"

She didn't even know what Kyle had been saying. It didn't even matter. The man's furrowed brow almost made her laugh.

"Wait, what—"

"Later," Roz said, reaching to close the laptop before he could protest. Once the laptop was closed, she answered her phone with a grin. "Naz, hey."

His voice was a dark, rich tenor coming through the speaker. A low note of music that danced over her skin with nothing more than two words.

"Morning, beautiful," he said.

Roz's heart jumped, and her smile grew wider. "That's ... quite a greeting."

"Yeah, but *true*."

This guy was something else.

"And I just wanted to say that," he added. "You busy tomorrow morning?"

She should have said yes, she would be busy. That she had to practice, and get her head back in the game. *Focus, focus, focus*. It should be her mantra.

Instead, she said, "Not busy at all."

"Great," Naz said, "I know a place."

# EIGHT

Naz scrubbed a hand over his face, and blinked up at the ceiling of his bedroom. He reached out to find the phone he'd left sitting on the nightstand the night before. His mind was only on one thing. He wanted to call Roz, and make sure she was still up for going out with him that morning.

"I forgot how lazy you can be in the mornings when you want to be," came a familiar voice from Naz's bedroom doorway.

If he hadn't been fully awake before, he sure as fuck was now.

Naz straightened in the bed like a rod had been driven into his spine, and forced him up. It sent the blanket around his body pooling at his waist. The man grinning in the doorway of the bedroom was lucky Naz had even bothered to throw on a pair of boxer-briefs the night before. Usually, he'd hit the bed fresh out of a fucking shower because he was too damn tired for anything else after running all day.

So was the life of a made man being mentored. Their life was not their own. It was now owned and controlled by whoever the fuck had a button in *Cosa Nostra*. Someone called, Naz answered. Someone needed something, then he had to go out and fucking get it for them.

Naz didn't mind a lot of the times. A made man was what he always wanted to be. Like his father, and his grandfathers. This life was as natural to him as breathing. It was bred into his very blood. He would be the fourth generation of Donati blood to be made—how the hell was he supposed to even consider something else?

"How did you get in my fucking place?" Naz demanded.

His father's lips quirked up at the edge, and Cross cocked a brow. There was no need for Naz to wonder where his attitude and arrogance came from when he had this man standing right across from him. From his looks to his mannerisms, and far too much in between … he was just like his father.

*Twins*, his mother would say.

Not entirely.

But damn close.

"Really," Cross murmured, giving his son *that* look, "you wonder how I got in here?"

"Without me knowing, *yes*."

Naz knew his father could pick a lock like nobody else. Cross just needed a few minutes, and some inspiration to get a door open. That didn't negate the fact Naz had his entire apartment *wired* to let him know if someone had gotten in while he slept.

Another benefit of being a genius, he supposed. All that work with electronics came in handy more often than it didn't.

"Nothing tripped when I got the door open, son," Cross said.

Naz's brow furrowed, and he did grab a hold of his phone, then. A quick check of an app he'd personally developed, tested, and installed for his security system told him that yeah, he hadn't even turned the final checks on the night before to set everything.

Well, *fuck*.

"Distracted?" his father asked.

Naz glanced sideways, and willed his father to shut up and stop asking questions. He didn't need an error like this pointed out to him at the moment. He had far too many other things on his mind, and he really couldn't afford to be off his game in life.

That only spelled bad things.

"Tired," Naz offered instead.

Cross nodded like he was considering that. "Zeke *did* have you running all over New York and back yesterday, didn't he?"

"More than usual, yeah."

"Suppose there's a reason for that?"

Naz stiffened as he started to move out of the bed. He took a brief moment to consider his father's words, and then went ahead with getting out of bed, and grabbing the clean slacks and dress shirt he'd left sitting in a garment bag after snatching it from the dry cleaners before he came home the night before.

His father said nothing as Naz shrugged on the shirt, and pulled up the pants. He let his son get dressed in peace, thankfully.

"I hadn't considered there was a reason he sent me running, no," Naz said. "He's your right-hand man, Dad. He's made—I'm *trying* to get the button. He can send me wherever he likes, at whatever time of day or night he likes. That is how this goes, right?"

Cross chuckled. "It is, yes."

"But now that you mention it …"

"He was in the next room when you called Roz yesterday morning. He also has cameras on his house … like every other made man in this state, Naz. And nobody missed how *close* you and she were at Cece's engagement party, son."

"So, my Godfather is trying to keep me away from his daughter. Is that what you're telling me?"

Cross grinned when Naz looked to him. "I think … well, I think he's trying to figure out what *you're* doing with his daughter. Or rather, what you plan on doing. Look at it like that, son."

Naz sucked air through his teeth. It was better than telling his father to let Zeke know he could go *fuck* himself straight up the closest wall he could find.

*Damn.*

That urge was strong, though. It kind of fucking shocked Naz how much he wanted to say it, too. Like the very idea of someone keeping Rosalynn away from him was going to make him do some kind of brilliant violence just because he could.

His father didn't miss it, either.

Cross knew him too well.

*I was you once*, his father liked to say every time he stepped in on one of Naz's plans to thwart them. His father always knew what he was going to do before he ever even did it. Most of the time, anyhow.

"Ah," his father murmured. "So, that's how it is, then."

"How *what* is?" Naz asked.

He focused his attention on buttoning up his shirt, and not looking at his father. It was easier, really.

"Roz," Cross said. "That's how it is with her, hmm?"

"Again, like—"

"You think you love her."

Naz's cheek twitched. An involuntary reaction at the word *think* coming out of his father's mouth in conjunction with his feelings for Roz. Like Naz didn't know what in the hell was going on inside his own mind.

"Not *think*," Naz muttered under his breath.

He didn't miss the way his father's brow lifted out of the corner of his eye, but he didn't turn to face him fully. Cross didn't seem to mind.

"You're sure?"

"Don't ask that," Naz countered, strolling into his walk-in closer to grab a pair of socks and shoes. "Don't *question* my mind. Don't ask me to explain what happens in my brain. I don't *do that*. I know what it knows, and *this* is what it knows."

That's just how his brain worked.

*Fucking genius thing again.*

And it knew from the second he looked at Roz who she was, and what he wanted with her. He wasn't going to apologize for that, or try to explain it.

"Must be confusing, that," Cross said, leaning against the door jamb with his arms crossed over his chest. "To just … turn around, and *bam*, there it is."

37

Naz slipped on the socks and shoes, before standing straight, facing his father, and giving him a smirk. Walking past Cross in the doorway, Naz said, "Must fucking be, huh?"

"Sometimes, you make me want to bust your mouth with that attitude."

Yet, his father never did. Never *once* even raised a hand to him. If anything, his father encouraged Naz to have a loud and opinionated voice. Demanded it of him, really. He made sure his son knew to never allow someone else's voice to overpower his just because he was younger, or anything of the sort.

Cross made a noise under his breath. "Just ... be the man I raised, Naz."

"I don't know how to be anything different, Dad."

"I know. *Zeke*, on the other hand ... well, he no longer has to figure you out as his godson, and this brilliant boy he watched grow up, Naz. He's got to figure you out as the young man who has suddenly found himself *very* interested in his seventeen-year-old daughter."

Naz hesitated in the hallway, even though his father was following close enough behind him to see the action. "Is that what it is—her age?"

Seventeen was legal in New York. He wasn't robbing a fucking cradle. The woman was old enough to make choices, according to the law. And hadn't she practically been living as a young adult for a while now?

"I don't think it's the age, really," Cross said, "more ... everything else."

"Everything else," Naz echoed.

His father walked past him in the hallway, and clapped him on the shoulder. "She's still his daughter. I know *you* don't understand, but I sure as hell do. Keep that in mind while he figures things out, too."

"Things like *what?*"

"Oh, Naz."

That time, his father patted him on the head like a *puppy*.

"For being so damn brilliant," his father said, smirking, "you're terribly fucking dense at times, son."

"Rude," Naz grunted.

"Yeah, well ... enjoy your breakfast with Roz," Cross said. "And don't ask how I know that, either."

Jesus Christ.

# NINE

Roz barely noticed her brother sitting at the kitchen table talking with her mother and father as she entered the room. Although, it really wasn't that unusual for her brother to show up at their parents' place at all hours of the day and night. Well, according to what her mother said when they talked on the phone.

She partly blamed it on the fact Luca was a momma's boy like nobody knew, but also on the fact her brother had just recently moved out. He wasn't used to not having his parents around, and he couldn't cook to save his life. He'd starve if it wasn't for their mother and drive-thrus.

None of that really mattered, though. Her mind was on someone else entirely as she prepped a tea, and scrolled through the last couple of messages on her phone from Naz.

*Be there by nine*, his last text said.

"Roz, are you going to eat breakfast with us, or keep staring at your phone?" Katya asked.

She glanced up from her phone, and gave her mother an apologetic smile. "I'm heading out for breakfast, actually."

Roz didn't miss the way her mother and father passed a look between one another. Katya only smiled in her soft way, while Zeke's gaze narrowed in on his daughter.

"Is that so?"

She shrugged. "Naz asked. I said yes."

She didn't miss the tic in her father's jaw at that statement. "You didn't think to ask me if that would be okay, or …?"

Roz laughed, and even Luca passed their father a look for that one. "Since when have you ever cared if I went out with someone for a date?"

"So, that is what it is, then."

"What?"

"A *date*," her father clarified.

"Zeke," Katya murmured. "Relax. It's *breakfast*."

"Today, Katya. *Today*, it is breakfast. Tomorrow it could be—"

"Whatever he asks me to do, *if* I want to do it," Roz interjected. "That's kind of how dating works, Daddy."

Zeke made a noise under his breath, but it was only the look his wife gave him that made her father turn to stare out the window in silence. Still, it kind of irked Roz a bit that her father was choosing to be difficult about something like dating *now*. That was new. Maybe because it was Naz?

She didn't know.

"Aren't you supposed to be practicing?" her brother asked. "Pretty sure I heard you on the phone this morning with ... what's his face."

Roz rolled her eyes. "*Kyle.*"

"That guy—yeah." Luca turned in his seat to look at her. "Isn't that what you told him you were doing *all morning*? Practicing."

"Why don't you mind your own business, Luca? God knows you don't need to be in *mine*."

Ouch.

She couldn't even try to hide the sharpness in her tone. No one at the table missed it, either, if the way they all turned to look at her was any indication.

"I told him what he wanted to hear," Roz said, refusing to meet any of their gazes, "because he won't leave me alone otherwise. I will practice when I get home. What difference does it make?"

Her brother shrugged. "Didn't say it made a difference. I just asked a question."

*Mmhmm.*

She believed that about as much as she believed the sky was fucking purple. She had no desire to call her brother out on his bullshit, and get in a verbal sparring match first thing in the morning, though, so she dropped it instead.

"You *do* need to get your focus on track," her mother said.

"Agreed," her father grumbled.

Roz shook her head. "I *am* on track."

That was a lie.

She wasn't able to focus at all when she sat down at the piano. Her mind was elsewhere. On the last text he sent. On the next one that might come through. The sound of his voice first thing in the morning. The way it *still* felt like his hand was holding hers, or that his kiss was on her lips days later.

Yeah, her focus was somewhere. But it certainly was not on the piano, or properly finishing the piece for the audition.

No doubt, it hadn't escaped her parents' notice. How could it when up until this point, nearly all of Roz's life had been dedicated to being the world's best pianist. She hadn't even bothered with making friends because friends meant time away from music, and practice, and *everything*.

"Sure," her mother said softly. "Just do what you need to do, yes? Whatever is best for you, sweetheart. We're going to support you no matter what. That's what we're here for. Isn't that right, Zeke?"

Katya passed her husband a look, and then Roz's father sighed with a nod.

"That's always been the case," her father said. "Whatever you need, Roz. You know that."

"Okay, so this morning … I need to go to breakfast without being made to feel guilty that I am having a life that doesn't involve me sitting on a piano bench."

There, she said it.

Let them make of it what they wanted.

Zeke grunted under his breath as something outside the window caught his attention. At the same time her phone buzzed, and a horn beeped outside, her father said, "Have a good breakfast, Roz."

Her phone said the same thing the beep of the horn essentially did, too. Naz was there, and waiting.

"Thank you, Daddy."

Zeke smiled. "Looks like Naz is here."

"And for once," Luca muttered, digging into his plate again, "he's not here for me."

"*Okay*," Roz drawled, giving her brother a glare that he couldn't even see, "that's enough of this. I'll see you all later."

"Be safe," her father called at her back.

"Zeke!"

"What, Katya?"

"Knock it *off*."

Her father's resounding grumble echoed behind Roz, but she just grinned and kept on walking. Grabbing her bag, a light jacket, and slipping on a pair of ballet flats at the door, she quickly exited the house.

And there he was.

Dark slacks.

White dress shirt.

*Leather jacket.*

And leaning against a BMW F 800 like the sportsbike was a fucking accessory on his arm or something. The black bike was all sleek lines, and hard curves. A lot like the man resting next to it with a lazy smile, and holding a helmet in both hands.

"Good, you wore jeans," he said. "I didn't want to tell you to change."

Roz was stuck between eyeing the beautiful bike, or the equally sexy man. Maybe *this* was why her father had looked out the window like he wanted to kill someone. It was very possible.

"Ever been on a bike?" Naz asked.

Roz shook her head. "Not even once."

"That's a fucking shame, girl."

"If I fell, my hands …"

41

Naz's easy smile slipped. "You could hurt your hands if you tripped over your own two feet getting out of bed in the morning, Roz."

"Yeah, I know."

"I can grab Luca's car, and trade my bike with him for the day, if you want." He gestured at her brother's Camaro parked beside their father's Lexus. "He's dying to try this baby out, so he won't mind."

Roz didn't even have to think about it. "No way."

Naz's brilliant, sinful smirk was back in an instant. "Yeah?"

Why not?

"No stunts," she warned.

With a wink, Naz saluted her with two fingers. "Scout's honor."

"You're far from a boy scout, Naz."

"But I'm *really good* at pretending to be one."

Roz laughed as she crossed the driveway, and took the helmet he offered in her own hands. "That's what counts, isn't it?"

Instead of answering, Naz leaned in and pressed a soft kiss to the side of her mouth. Quick, and gentle, it was over before it even began. And yet, that simple, fast kiss lit up a whole fire inside her body.

It made her breath quicken, and her heart race like nothing else.

"Morning," he said, still staying close enough that the dark brown of his eyes was the only thing she could see. "Since, you know, I didn't get to tell you that when you first came out."

Roz wet her lips, and grinned. "Morning to you, too."

"Don't be scared of the bike, yeah?" He shrugged in that way of his that spoke of easy confidence and a laid-back demeanor. All things Naz *radiated*, she thought. "Never be scared of the bike, Roz. Not while I'm driving it, anyway."

"I'm not scared of the bike."

"Good."

He kissed her again, then, but it wasn't fast, gentle, or anything like the first. It was hard, deep, and *lingering*. His hand came up to grab the back of her neck to pull her closer, and all she could do was take him in. She could only give in to the sweep of his tongue demanding she open up for him, and lose herself in the way he practically handed over his soul when he kissed her.

He was like Novocain to her senses. Numbing, and *wonderful*. He lit her up like fireworks, and everything else was nothing more than background noise. A buzz—*numbing*.

She wasn't scared of the bike.

The man on it, though …

Well, he terrified her.

But in a really good way.

# TEN

Naz might have kept driving past the small roadside breakfast truck despite how hungry he was simply because he was *loving* the way Roz had wrapped her arms around his body, and was squeezing for all she was worth. He didn't think it was from fear, either. He had comms set up in the helmets, but he'd kept them shut off. So, the drive had been quiet between the two of them. He didn't really need words when he could *feel* her, though.

At the sight of the brightly colored food truck parked where it did every morning—never failed—, Naz pulled the sportsbike off the road smoothly. Even as he found a spot to park the bike, shut off the engine, and dropped down the kickstand, Roz still didn't let him go.

It was only once he tugged off his helmet did her arms finally unravel from around his middle. He stepped off the bike, and turned to help her with her own helmet. Her mess of wavy hair spilled around her shoulders, and a bright smile lit up her face.

Naz laughed. "Fun, right?"

Roz made a noise. "I mean ... *scary* might be a better word. At first, anyway."

"I thought you weren't scared of the—"

"I *wasn't*." She poked him right in the middle of his chest, making Naz laugh when she mock glared. "And then you had to go and pop up on one tire *twice*."

"I had to hit the fuel! You know, to get the fuck out of the way of people trying to cut *in front of us*."

She gave him another one of those looks. Naz only shrugged. He actually wasn't lying. That was the thing about driving a bike on the highway. Fucking *nobody* looked for a bike. They just merged without looking, and a bike rider had to be careful.

*Dress for the fall, not the ride.*

There was a reason that whole saying had come about, after all.

"They don't look for us, is all," Naz said. "So, defensive driving it is."

Roz sighed, and smiled but still looked away from him like she didn't know what she wanted to do with him in that moment. Naz didn't blame

43

her. Half the time, he didn't know what in the hell he wanted to do with himself.

So was his life.

Reaching out, he caught one of her stray waves of hair between his forefinger, and thumb. He curled the strand around his finger just because he could. *Damn.* He hadn't realized how soft and silky her hair was. He had the strongest urge to just thrust both of his hands into those waves, grab tight, and *fucking kiss her.*

He didn't know what she would think of that.

He settled for tucking the strand behind her ear, and then he pulled away. But not before letting his fingertips drift over the shell of her ear, and then across her cheek, too. It pulled a sweet, soft smile from her lips as her sky-blue eyes turned back on him again. Her teeth cut into those pink lips as she watched him for a moment.

"It was fun, though," she murmured.

Naz smirked. "I know. Anytime you want a ride, baby, you let me know."

He hadn't realized how the words could be taken in different ways until they left his mouth, but hey, it was out there now. There was no fucking taking it back. Besides … it wasn't a goddamn lie, either.

Roz's cheeks pinked with just a touch of color. "Will do. So, are we taking a break for a minute before we get back on the road, or …?"

"Nope."

"No?"

Naz turned so he could rest against the bike while Roz was still straddling the back seat. He pointed to the food truck just across the road from where he had parked. Famous for its sugary breakfast treats, the truck—one of several across the United States for this company—only made food from five till eleven in the morning, and then they shut down for the day. They were *so* popular, and the food was so good that they had a social media following that rivaled celebrities.

Already, there was a line of people for the truck going all the way down the road. People didn't mind waiting to get their fill. Some even traveled quite a ways just to get a taste of whatever the food truck made.

And this particular truck?

Well … Naz knew the guy.

Old friends.

Roz gave him a look. "I thought you were taking me out somewhere to eat."

He gave her a grin. "This food is better than *sex*, Roz."

Her cheeks did that *pink* thing again. He wasn't going to act like he didn't like the sight of it because he did. He liked it even more that he was the cause. He wondered just how often he could get her to do that, and just how far that blush extended down her neck and chest when she was breathless, and so fucking close to coming.

*Damn.*

Wow.

His mind went there *fast*.

Naz's grin deepened. "I mean, any sex I've ever had, anyway. I'll let you know if that changes soon, huh?"

He didn't miss the way her gaze darkened, or how her smile turned a little shy and yet still sly at the same time. He didn't know how in the hell someone could manage that, but she *did*. Yeah, he was definitely going to make her do that more often.

"Well, *I* wouldn't know," Roz said, her tone coming out a little too nonchalant. "About sex, I mean."

Naz glanced at her again, realizing what she was telling him without actually telling him. And shit, he hadn't been expecting that at all. "Really?"

Roz shrugged. "Nope."

A virgin.

That wasn't Naz's usual style, at all. And yet … he *liked* it. Maybe because it was her, and that meant no one had come before him. No one had ever touched this girl. She was fucking perfect in every sense of the word.

That drove him even more crazy.

Like he needed that.

Roz's cheeks were pink again, but she acted like they weren't at all when she said, "Are we going to eat, or …?"

"Yep. Care to let me pick for you?"

She eyed the long line for the truck once more. "I think by the time you get us food, my stomach will have eaten itself from waiting for so long."

Naz chuckled, and pushed off the bike before turning to face her. "Oh, Roz, I don't have to *wait*. Not for this truck, anyway. My buddy owns it. Got him out of a scrape once. We're friends, you could say."

"What does that mean? You could say?"

It meant a lot of things.

Mostly, his last name afforded him things.

That was another topic for another day. Today was not that day, as far as he was concerned.

"Can I pick for you, then?" he asked instead of answering.

Roz smiled. "Yeah, surprise me."

"You got it, sweetheart."

Naz darted forward, and dropped a quick kiss to Roz's smiling lips just to see that pink hue color her cheeks again before he winked, and spun on his heels. *Food it was …*

His mind was on everything else *but* food when it came to Roz. But fucking food it was.

Naz damn near groaned at the sight of Roz taking the bite of waffle from his fingertips. Covered in powdered sugar, whipped cream, and drizzled with a mixture of chocolate, *real* maple syrup, and melted caramel, he thought the truck's waffles were the best thing they sold.

Roz chewed the bite, and a soft moan escaped her lips. Between those little noises crawling out of her throat, the teasing grin on her mouth, and the fact she was still straddling his bike as he fed her … well, that right there was enough to test Naz's very carefully maintained control.

Suddenly, he had no fucking control at all.

Not when it came to her.

"Okay, you're right," she said, "yours is good, too."

"Better than yours was?"

Roz shrugged. "Pretty equal. They're both basically diabetes on a plate. Do you eat this *every* morning?"

"Four times a week," Naz returned easily. "It's faster just to grab something like this when I'm up at all hours of the day on the go for somebody else. Anyone can call, and I have to go."

Roz's brow furrowed like she was about to ask him what he meant, but that was not a conversation Naz wanted to have right now, so he opted to just distract her. And by *distract her*, he meant using the pad of his thumb to wipe away the powdered sugar left over on her lips.

Also, maybe it wasn't so much a distraction for her as the fact he *really* just wanted to touch her lips. Feel them, and fucking *taste* them.

Roz stilled as his thumb swiped over her lips with a soft touch, and then her tongue followed the same path as he pulled away. He couldn't help but stick his thumb between his own lips to suck off the powdered sugar he wiped away.

Her cheeks pinked again.

*Yes.*

"You're something else, Nazio Donati," Roz whispered.

"Something good, though."

That was most certainly his cockiness coming out to play, but it was what it was. He'd been raised by the best, and he was just *born* the fucking best.

Why pretend differently?

Roz leaned forward, and used her hands on the seat to keep her balance as she came closer to him. There was a glitter to her gaze—something sly and sweet that made him want to come closer, so he did just that by inching forward until the two of them were close enough that he could see the flecks of darker blue closer to her irises.

"Do you know what I expected for today?" she asked.

Naz tipped his chin down. "Not particularly."

"I thought ... fancy restaurant, the usual."

"That wouldn't have been bad, either."

Roz shook her head. "Not at all."

"We can do that next time," he offered.

"Next time?"

"We're just getting started here, Roz."

"This was perfect. *Really*." She smiled in that way again. "I should have known better than to expect the *usual* with you."

"Why's that?"

"You're not at all a *usual* man, Naz."

"I'm not anything spectacular, either."

Beyond the whole genius thing, he was just a man at the end of every day. The same as any other man, he supposed.

Roz arched a brow. "You know, I doubt that."

She leaned up just enough to catch his mouth with a kiss. She still tasted sweet like the powdered sugar on the waffles, but there was something far more sinful on her lips, too. This girl somehow managed to quiet all of Naz's overactive thoughts with nothing more than a press of her lips, and the tease of her tongue sliding in to war with his. All the while, those eyes of hers stayed locked on his.

He was still kind of hungry.

Not so much for food, though.

He dropped what was left of the waffle just so he could get his hands on Roz instead. *That's* what he needed.

Her.

# ELEVEN

Roz heard the final notes of the ballad echo into the room, but she didn't really *feel* the music. Not like she usually would, anyway. Her mind was otherwise distracted. On something else entirely that didn't include the shiny top of a piano, and ivory keys under her fingertips. She went through the motions of playing the song because she had to—practice, practice, practice was the mantra—but not because she was really *feeling* it.

"That's … better," she heard Kyle say quietly.

Roz glanced up from the keys of the piano to find the man watching her from the screen of the laptop. She'd been going through this same song— the one she intended to use for the Australia audition—for *two hours*. He wouldn't let her play anything else. Not even to warm up her fingers. *This* was what she needed to play, he said.

Until she felt it in her bones.

Until she could *breathe* the fucking notes.

Until she thought about nothing else but this.

That was kind of hard to do when Rosalynn's mind was entirely filled with something else now. She was far too busy lately thinking about Naz, and the next time she was going to get to see him or talk to him instead of playing the piano and preparing for this fucking audition.

And the bigger problem?

It wasn't a problem for her at all.

She *knew* she was distracted. She knew her mind wasn't in the right place. She knew her focus was *gone*.

She just didn't see the problem.

Why was it such a bad thing that Roz was learning there were other things in the world to enjoy other than a fucking piano, and making music? Couldn't she just enjoy this for a while?

"The song is good," Kyle said again.

Roz sighed. "Thank you."

As her mother would tell her, always thank someone when they give you a compliment. Even if it's the very last thing you want to do. Kill them with kindness was her mother's mantra.

"It's not the song, though," her mentor added after a beat of silence, "it's the person playing it. *You*, obviously."

Roz's jaw clenched, but if Kyle saw it he didn't say. She didn't want her irritation to be clear to him, anyway. She didn't want him figuring out there *was* something distracting her. His first and last mission at that point would be to remove Roz from the situation. To demand she return back to school, and the rigid structure of dorm life.

And no matter how many times she refused, he would still make it happen. That's what a good mentor was supposed to do, anyway. Keep her on track, and make sure she was doing what she needed to do to get where she wanted to go with her career. He made the tough decisions, and whether she liked it or not, she would follow his demands.

The last thing Roz wanted right now—or ever—was to be taken away from Naz. Why would she want that when she was just getting to know him really?

Even if it felt like her heart had known him her whole life.

Even if she *had* known him her whole life …

They were just getting started.

"The person playing it has not yet learned to *love* it," Kyle said quietly. "Or, that's what it looks like to me, Rosalynn. You're not putting yourself in the music. Why the detachment? You spent months composing this piece. It is your work come to *life*. These notes should be embedded in your bones, and for whatever reason, you look like a damn robot going through the motions right now. *Why?*"

Roz shrugged.

It was the best she could offer.

Not good enough for Kyle, though. Roz didn't need him to say it for her to know. And if he didn't tell her today, he would soon enough. That was a promise.

When she didn't speak, Kyle just continued on like nothing was wrong to begin with, saying, "I noticed you changed the third stanza, and a bit of the chorus since the last time we went through it in its entirety."

Which was last week …

The day before Naz took Roz out to breakfast for the first time. Every day after, he'd shown up at her parents' house with that bike, his fucking grin, and a promise to do something fun. He never failed in finding something fun for them to do, either.

And it usually ended the same way with Roz wanting to kiss the man until she could no longer breathe while his hands held her tight, and he was all she could think about or feel. That's how it always ended.

"It's … softer," Kyle said. "The music, I mean. Sexier, even, if I wanted to use that word. Your notes go low and slow. *Soft* for a moment, and then it lingers in that stanza. You speed it up, but barely. It feels like a heartbeat, doesn't it? A heart that's *exploding*."

Roz laughed. "You're looking too deep into it, Kyle. It's just a few tweaks."

He wasn't looking too deep into it, actually, but she didn't want to tell him that. If she did, then he would ask what brought on the changes. That would lead into Naz, and once again, Kyle would figure out her distraction and pull the fucking plug on her being in New York until the audition.

Nonetheless, Kyle wasn't wrong. The music *had* changed. Slight tweaks, but any musician knew that slight tweaks to anything meant something creatively was different for the person writing the music.

Naz was the reason why her music was changing. She felt differently around him. He made her mind light up like nothing else, and her heart *did* feel like it was about to explode every time he fucking touched her.

How could her music not change when she knew this kind of thing existed?

"Tweaks that absolutely made it better," Kyle said, "but *why* is the better question. And why, if you're making it better with these tweaks are you not *feeling* it like you usually do, Roz? Are you sure New York is where you want and need to be right now to prepare for this audition?"

"Never been surer," she lied.

Well, was it a lie?

If she left, then she was going to constantly think about what could have been between her and Naz. She'd be distracted with all the things she left behind. All the things left unsaid.

That felt just as bad as *this*.

Roz figured she might as well be distracted and happy, than distracted and *unhappy*.

Kyle sighed loudly on the screen when he realized he wasn't getting a straight answer from Roz, and she wasn't talking more than she had to. "You don't have much longer to get this *right*, Roz. What if I came down to New York, do you think that would—"

"I would rather take this time alone, Kyle."

"Fine. Same time tomorrow, then?"

She wanted to say no.

Instead, she muttered, "Same time tomorrow, yep."

Where else was she going to be?

Apparently, right fucking here.

Roz was still sitting at her piano an hour later when a throat cleared, and drew her attention to the doorway. Her father leaned in, and gave her a smile.

"You seem … distracted," he noted.

*Great.*

Back to this again.

"I'm fine," she said. "Just thinking."

"Mmm, I heard you up here playing. It was good. Did you change a bit of it? Sounds different, *dushka.*"

She grinned at her father's use of the Russian word for a term of endearment. He was so far from Russian that it wasn't even funny. One of the *most* Italian men she had ever met in her life, but her mother was Russian through and through. Katya's pet name for Roz lived on—none of the Italian ones seemed to stick.

"It felt like it needed a change," Roz said. "I could tell it did, but I'm not into it, at the same time."

"Because of the changes?"

"No. I'm just not in the mood."

Her father stiffened a bit. "Not in the mood to play the piano. That's what you mean."

Roz nodded. "I guess, yeah."

"Is that maybe because you've been doing practically everything else with a certain someone instead of working on this piece for the audition? Maybe a certain someone is taking up a little too much space in your mind, and your music is taking a hit, Roz."

*Jesus.*

"Maybe that's fine, too," Roz countered.

"Is it?" her father asked, his tone never changing from that same calm tone. He always used that on her when he thought she was doing something wrong, but didn't want to come right out and say so. Roz wasn't stupid. She knew how her father worked. "Is it fine when your dream from the time you were just two years old was to play piano on the biggest stage you could find for anyone and everyone to hear you, Roz? Is it fine if that no longer matters because a *boy* caught your attention for a moment?"

*Ouch.*

"I didn't say it didn't *matter,*" she snapped.

Zeke arched a brow. Her father was not a loud man. He'd never even yelled at his children as they grew up. But disrespect? No, he never stood for that.

"Try again," he said, "and with a touch less attitude this time, Rosalynn Katya Puzza."

Damn.

Full name, too.

"It's not that it doesn't matter," she said quietly, "I just …"

Zeke softened in his posture when his daughter couldn't come up with the right words to say. He pressed gently with a soft, "What is it?"

"I just want to figure this out."

"And what is *this*?"

"Naz," she said simply.

What he was to her.

Why he made her feel so crazy.

How he could affect her *this much*.

She needed to understand.

"Do you think maybe because he's the first boy—"

"You keep calling him a boy, but … he's definitely *not*," Roz said, smiling a little.

Zeke grunted under his breath. "No, he's certainly a young man. But did you know I was the one who helped his father cut his cord when he was born in their bed because they couldn't make it to the hospital in time? I was the one who held him while his father helped his mother as they waited for the ambulance, Rosalynn. He may be a young man to you, but he will always be the boy I watched grow up, and I won't apologize for it, either."

"So, he only becomes a man when he gets a little too close to me, and you get stuck in your feelings about it, right?"

Her father didn't even *try* to hide it. "I'm working on it. I also see my very driven and talented daughter being entirely messed up over him … putting her ambitions and goals to the sidelines because he's forefront and center. And that makes me pause, too."

"Can't I just figure it out?" she asked. "It's not because he's the first guy I noticed. It's because he's *him*, Daddy."

Zeke tilted his head to the side a bit. "And you're you, Roz."

"What?"

"Never forget that you are *you*. And you are as equally as amazing as he is, but for entirely different reasons. Don't lose what makes you amazing because you're so caught up in what makes him amazing to you."

Roz wanted to respond, but her phone rang with a familiar tune. One she put for Naz's phone number. Her father didn't miss it when he gave her a look, and then turned to leave the room.

"Don't keep him waiting," her father murmured. "How else can you practice later if you don't get him out of your system today, hmm?"

Well, then …

# TWELVE

Naz tugged his beanie down over his head as his mother followed him down the hallway. "Nah, just put a plate in the fridge, Ma, in a container. I'll grab it before I head out. Promise."

Catherine sighed. "I can't believe you're not staying long enough to have *supper*, Naz. You're heading out tomorrow, right? I know your run is coming up. You always spend an evening with us before heading out for that."

His mother wasn't wrong. It was something his father had gotten him in to the habit of doing. Before each and every gun run he made, Naz spent the evening with his family. *Like a reminder*, his dad would say. *This is where you need to come back to, Naz. This is where you're wanted and needed. So, you remind yourself why you need to get this done, and get back safely*.

So, he'd come.

But he also had someone else to go see, too.

"But—"

"Catty," came a dark murmur from down the hallway.

Naz glanced over his shoulder to find his father leaning lazily in the doorway between the hallway and the living room. Cross had said nothing about Naz leaving early because it looked like he expected it.

His mother, on the other hand …

"Let him go," Cross said. "He's got business across the woods, I imagine."

Catherine glanced between her husband, and her son for a moment before her posture softened. "Oh. Why didn't you just say that?"

Naz shrugged, but said nothing.

Because it wasn't anyone's business, he supposed. This thing between him and Roz was still all-consuming, and a little too crazy. He hadn't even figured it out yet. He was not willing to share it, either. Not even with his mother. Not right now.

Catherine would understand eventually.

"Say hello for us," his mother whispered, patting his cheek with a soft touch. "And *do not* forget your food before you go."

Naz laughed, and leaned in to kiss his mother's waiting cheek. "How can I forget your cooking, Ma?"

She gave him *that* look. All mother's had it.

He just laughed again.

With a wave, Naz was free to leave without more questions, apparently. Why his mother didn't just realize where he was going as he'd headed for the *back* of the house, and not the front, Naz didn't know.

He tightened the neck on his leather jacket, and slipped out into the evening light. It wasn't entirely dark out, since the moon was up on one side while the sun was still peeking out a bit on the other side. Just enough light to make the trip on foot through the woods a bit safer.

Naz *could* have pushed the gun run back a couple of days, but that meant doing a run to Mexico and crossing the border with the guns on a weekday instead of the following weekend. That always made shit a little more complicated, and dangerous, really. Every run he made was carefully planned, and executed according to schedule to minimize the risk of a smuggle going bad.

That was his father's first and last lesson when Naz decided he was going to follow Cross's footsteps into gunrunning.

One of many lessons, really.

*But* ... he'd been trained by the best which may not have made Naz the very best there was, but he was terribly fucking close to it. There wasn't another gunrunner on the continent that could challenge Naz's success rates. Except maybe his father, and frankly, Naz was getting close to passing that record, too.

Not that Cross liked it pointed out.

Everybody had their pride.

Despite how badly Naz had wanted to push the run back a couple of days so that he could spend more time with Roz—the run was going to keep him away for a week, likely, with no contact to anyone outside of his partner and the buyer—he figured it was just best to get it the hell over with.

He could pick up with Roz once he got back. She'd understand, even if he didn't plan on telling her running guns was what he would be doing for the next week instead of being here with her.

That was a conversation for another day.

Not tonight.

Slipping into the trails, Naz navigated the terrain easily. Like it was the back of his hand he was recalling, and not a dirt path. He could walk these trails with his eyes closed, likely. He knew them that well, and felt that comfortable with them.

He was halfway through the trail when he caught sight of her coming down the path from the other direction. Naz's grin split his face instantly. Roz was still looking down at her feet, so she hadn't even noticed him at all yet. Likely making sure she didn't trip over something knowing her.

Those hands of hers …

Those damn hands.

So precious.

Soft.

Delicate.

Full of talent, spirit, and *his*.

She was entirely his.

He'd decided.

"Sometimes, you need to watch for what's coming *down* the path, too, Roz," Naz said, smirking, "or someone might sneak up on you like this."

Roz's head snapped up, and she came to a full stop only inches from where Naz was standing with that shit-eating smirk. She blinked, smiled widely, and then launched herself at him. Naz caught her around the waist with a laugh of his own, before picking her right up from the ground like she weighed nothing at all.

Her legs wrapped around his waist, and that thin, flimsy dress she wore did nothing to hide the soft warmth of her center pressing against his stomach. It was fucking impossible for him to ignore the way it felt, never mind how it had his cock perking up in an instant. Like the bastard was revving and ready to go. His dick just wanted to say hello, and get acquainted with the parts of Roz that he'd been holding back from because this … and that, would always be on her time.

When *she* wanted.

No matter what.

"I said I would come over to your place," he murmured, reaching up to stroke her cheek with two fingers. He took the moment of her silence to enjoy the sight the of her joy coloring her cheeks, and making her eyes glitter. Nothing was more beautiful than this woman. He was sure of it. Life, and beauty, and grace right there in his arms. He was holding it—*her*. Nothing could make him let go. He was sure of it. "What, did you get tired of waiting?"

Roz let out a breathless laugh as her legs tightened around his waist, and she dropped a sweet kiss to his mouth. "Nope. Just wanted to surprise you."

Naz tucked a strand of her loose hair behind her ear. "That so?"

"Yep."

"Missed you, my girl."

"You just saw me yesterday."

So?

Was that supposed to make a difference because Naz didn't think so. He couldn't control the way he fucking felt all the time when it came to this woman. Even a second away from her was one second too many, as far as he was concerned.

He wasn't going to apologize for it, either.

"Besides," he said, "I think you *like* it when I miss you."

Winking, he spun them around so that her back was resting against the smooth trunk of a tree. Leaning in, he kissed a path across her smiling cheekbone, and then down to her lips. Over her chin, and jaw. Finally, down her throat. Soft, slow kisses that allowed him to feel the way she shivered, and drew in quick, short breaths.

*God*, yeah.

He liked that.

Slowly, Naz came back to her mouth before lingering there a little longer with his next kiss. So then, he could *taste* her. Feel the heat of her mouth, and enjoy the way their kiss had somehow become a familiar dance for him.

Roz grew silent, and her gaze locked on his. Her soft fingertips came up to stroke overtop the dusting of facial hair covering his jaw and cheeks. There was something in her eyes—something he *knew* because it reflected back in his. He wore that same look from the moment he laid eyes on her, and really *saw* her.

Still, he stayed quiet.

Unmovable.

This was all on her.

"I think I more than like it, actually," Roz whispered.

"Oh?"

"Love it, maybe."

Naz quirked a brow high. "Is that what this is—*love?*"

"Isn't that a little crazy, Naz?"

"What, to be in love?"

"Maybe."

"I'd rather be crazy than *normal*, Roz," Naz returned. "And you're far from normal, aren't you?"

"Like you, too."

"Mmm. Better we're crazy together. It's more fun this way."

She swallowed audibly, and then her tongue peeked out to swipe across her bottom lip. Naz couldn't help himself but to trace the same path her tongue had taken with the pad of his thumb. That gaze of hers—still locked on him and *waiting*, now—darkened, and he felt her bottom lip tremble under his touch.

He drew his hand away, but her voice stopped him. Airless, and aching. That's how she sounded to him.

"Don't stop *now*," Roz said softly.

"Roz—"

Her legs tightened around him in that way again. The way that made her lower half press firmly against him. There was no hiding the hard ridge of his cock rubbing against the soft junction between her thighs, either.

"*Fuck*," Naz mumbled. "Don't start that out here."

"Why not?"

"Because I'm *not* fucking you against a tree." Naz's smirk came back in an instant. "At least, not for your *first* time."

Her cheeks pinked, and her lips popped open.

"That's not how this should be," he added quieter, drawing closer to the sweetness that was her mouth. "That's never how your first time should be, Roz."

"Shouldn't it be how *I* want it to be?"

Naz chuckled. "No, what you want right now is to soothe the fucking ache, babe. You want to feel better. It's called relief and *release*. That's what you want. You think that's sex, but it can be *a lot* of things."

"I know what release is, Nazio."

His grin deepened. "Oh, do you now?"

That pink color climbed down her throat. It only made Naz's cock harder, really. "Well—"

He leaned closer until their noses touched, she couldn't see anything but him, and his lips grazed hers as he said, "because you touch yourself, don't you? You get yourself *off*, Roz. Is that how you know?"

She sucked in a sharp breath.

Naz wasn't about to let her be shy now. Not two minutes ago, she had been more than willing to try and fuck him in the woods. She had it in her—she just needed a little help to bring the wild out.

Naz was damn good at being *wild*.

"Tell me," he murmured. "What do you think about when you're touching yourself, hmm? Go on, *tell me*."

Roz blinked. "You."

"Me."

"You," she echoed. "I think about you, and it makes me *shake*."

Hell yeah, that's what he wanted to hear.

His lips crashed against hers hard. There was nothing nice or soft or easy about the kiss. Gone was the way he wanted to taste and enjoy the moment. How could he give a shit about that when her fingernails were digging into his jaw as she pulled him impossibly closer, and kissed him back like it was the breath she needed in her lungs to *live*.

It was addictive.

*Amazing.*

So fucking crazy.

His hands had a mind of their own. Skimming under the skirt of her dress to push the flimsy fabric higher around her thighs, so his fingers could inch closer to heaven. Roz's teeth nipped into his lower lip before she pulled that beanie from his head to get her hands wrapped up in his hair.

His fingertips found her warm and damp overtop her cotton panties. Unashamed and *fucking perfect*, she ground against the feeling of his hand stroking her where she wanted him the most.

Where had that shyness gone now?

Naz was glad it left.

Her hand came down to meet with his before slipping beneath her panties. The wet heat of her sex met his fingertips. Slick, and so fucking sleek. The soft, trimmed hair grazed his palm as she pressed her body harder against his hand.

"*More,*" Roz demanded.

Christ.

He couldn't possibly deny her when she sounded like that. His fingers found her sweetest spot—tight, warm and wet. And he felt her own hand circle and press and *stroke*. Until she was shaking, mumbling his name, and looking sweeter than ever.

Roz really did make the best kind of music.

# THIRTEEN

The blank screen of Roz's phone was taunting her. She was sure of it. The longer she stared at it and willed it to light up with a call or message, the more it seemed determined to do absolutely nothing for her.

Three days.

Three *long days*.

That's how long it had been since Roz received even a simple text message from Naz. Every call she made to him went to voicemail, and every text went unanswered. She was trying really hard not to be pissed off, but it was fucking *hard*.

You know, considering the last time they'd spoken was when he lowered her to the ground after having his hands shoved down her freaking panties. That wasn't really the best time to skip out on somebody, and if that's what he was doing, then Naz was a *jerk*.

To say the least.

Glaring at the phone again, Roz tossed it to the table, huffed, and crossed her arms over her chest. Wasn't it bad enough that just the fact he hadn't answered her texts and calls put her on edge in a whole new way? Before, she couldn't concentrate on her music *because* Naz was around. Now, she couldn't fucking concentrate on anything because she was wondering why he wasn't around.

This was not what Roz wanted.

At all.

Nobody ever said love was like a goddamn disease. Like an infection ravaging someone's entire soul and heart until there was nothing left to keep for yourself. But that's exactly what it was like, and Roz wasn't sure if she was made out for this.

Slowly, like an urge she couldn't control, her gaze slid back in the direction of the discarded phone. Before she could stop herself, Roz reached out and snatched it up from the table once more just so she could check again.

Even though she knew it was still blank.

Nothing was there.

She knew, and she still had to check.

Yep.

*Just like a disease.*

He made her lovesick, and now she was *dying.*

Unlocking the screen, Roz brought up the texts, and sent one more to Naz just because she could. It wasn't *all* anger that she was feeling. There was a hell of a lot of worry mixed in, too. It wasn't like him to go off the grid like this.

Sure, he'd said he would be busy with work for a while, but what exactly did that mean? He'd told her that before, and usually, he called her back by the end of the night, or better yet, showed up at her house with that grin she liked far too much.

Not this time, though.

It just felt … off.

Roz typed out a quick text, and sent the message off. *What the hell, Naz? Where are you?*

She wasn't the type of girl that blew up a guy's phone. Frankly, she never found a guy she gave a shit about enough to do that, anyway. Naz apparently wasn't the same, and while she was sure she would regret all these texts and messages later … well, right now she was just worried and pissed and *wondering.*

"You okay over there?"

Roz's head snapped up, and she found her mother leaning against the kitchen island while she nursed a cup of coffee. "Yeah, fine, Ma."

Katya nodded. "Mmhmm. How long do you think I was standing here?"

*God, please don't say more than a couple of seconds.*

"I don't know," Roz hedged.

"Five minutes," her mom murmured.

Well, fuck her whole life.

"He's not calling you back, or what?" Katya asked.

Roz sighed. "It doesn't—"

"It does matter, or you would leave your phone alone, yes?" Kayta raised her eyebrows as if to dare her daughter to deny it. Roz chose to stay silent. That was her best defense when words wouldn't work. And very rarely did words work when it came to her mother. Katya never fell for that kind of thing. "Maybe he's just … busy? He is a very active young man, Rosalynn. I'm sure he's not out doing something you—"

"I don't think he's with someone else, if that's what you're trying to say," Roz was quick to interject. "I just don't know where he is, or why he won't answer my calls."

Her mother nodded. "Hmm, did you ask your brother?"

"Called him this morning."

"And?"

"And he said Naz was working. That was it. *Working.*"

Which told Roz nothing, and left her with more questions than answers. Actually, that was when the anger started to bleed away, and her concern really picked up. If it was just work, then her brother should have been able to give her more information, right? Why couldn't Naz find five freaking seconds to call her back?

None of this made sense.

Katya sighed quietly. "You're sure Luca said Naz was working?"

"I'm not *deaf*, Ma." Her mother gave her that look, and Roz was quick to check her attitude. "Sorry."

Katya pressed her lips together, and then hummed under her breath. Setting the cup aside on the counter, she pointed a finger at Roz and then said, "Give me a few minutes. Maybe I can help. But keep that bad mood for *him*, yeah? Not your mother, *dushka*."

Roz smirked. "Got it, Ma."

She didn't know how exactly her mother planned to help, but it didn't matter. Roz was distracted by staring at her phone again, and wondering. Love really was like a fucking sickness she couldn't shake.

Maybe because it was a first love.

Her first love.

Was it supposed to feel like this?

All crazy and heavy and *fragile*.

Like if she breathed the wrong way, she was going to fall apart at the seams?

*God.*

"Get your jacket on, and let's go," came a new voice from the kitchen doorway.

Roz found her father standing there with a set of car keys hanging from his fingertips. Zeke flashed a smile, but Roz stayed put.

"What, why?"

"We're going to go visit someone," her father said. "And I didn't ask for questions. I told you to do something. Get to it."

Roz gave her father a side eye, but despite his words, his tone was joking in nature. Zeke flashed another smile, and twirled the keys around his finger. Another silent demand for her to hurry up, and get moving.

She got her ass up from the table, and moved.

"I thought you said we were going to visit someone," Roz said, glancing over at her dad.

Zeke shrugged, and cut the engine on the car. "We are. Cross and Catherine."

Roz's gaze narrowed. "But why?"

"Because they're my friends, and your godparents."

"And because Ma told you to take me out of the house and do something with me?"

Probably her mother's way of thinking she could get Roz's mind off Naz. That was highly unlikely given this was his *parents'* home and all.

"No, that wasn't what she said at all. I promise you that, Roz."

Zeke didn't offer anything more before he got out of the car, and slammed the door. Bending down, he looked in and pointed at her door as if to silently say, *Let's go.*

She got out of the car, and raced after her father to catch up with him. He didn't even bother to ring the doorbell before he opened the door, and walked right into the large Donati home. Echoing laughter came from down the hall before Catherine darted between the living room, into the hallway, and then disappeared into the kitchen. Her husband was fast on her heels.

"Get back here, Catty!"

"No way. I am keeping that picture *forever.*"

"Jesus Christ, woman—"

"Save the foreplay for when the guests are gone, yeah?" Zeke shouted.

Cross was the first one to come back out from the kitchen by poking his head into the hallway first. The dark-eyed man narrowed his gaze on Roz's father. "Don't you know how to fucking knock, or what?"

"You don't knock at my house."

"That's fair," Cross murmured with a shrug. Then, his gaze drifted to Roz. "And you brought Roz along. Did I forget something, or—"

"Someone is missing someone else, actually," her father said vaguely.

Cross's brow shot up as his gaze turned on her again. Roz felt the way her cheeks heated up, but she settled for glaring at her father. Zeke acted like nothing was wrong.

"Figured she could use some company, and then maybe she'll, you know, get out of her mood," Zeke said.

"Stop it," Roz muttered under her breath.

Cross chuckled. "Roz, Catherine is in the kitchen finishing up some tarts, if you want one."

Roz's face was as red as a goddamn tomato. She was sure of it. Nonetheless, she was still grateful for the chance to escape the situation, so she nodded, and mumbled a quick thanks before darting ahead of her father.

Once she was in the kitchen, that didn't stop the voices from filtering in from the hallway even as they tried to keep quiet. Catherine shot Roz a sly grin that said she knew the girl was spying but didn't give a single shit either way. The woman was good like that.

"I take it he didn't tell her," Zeke said. "Don't you think maybe he should have?"

"It's Naz's business when and how he wants to deal with his *business* but especially when it comes to Rosalynn, Zeke. Let him tell her why he goes off like this on his own time, and when he's ready to."

"That's shitty for her, then. She's stuck *wondering*. And where did my fucking daughter go, huh? I swear the only goddamn thing she thinks about now is *your son*."

Cross grunted under his breath. "Say that like it's a bad thing one more time, man. Do it."

"Jesus." Her father sighed. "It's not a *bad thing*, Cross. It's Nazio. It's not bad. I don't ... mean that it's bad."

"I know what you mean."

"Then act like it," Zeke countered.

"Let them figure this out on their own. This fucking ... love thing. *Them*. Let them figure it out on their own time and way. Including Nazio, and business."

"*Fine*."

"You're such a prick."

"I'm allowed to be right now," Zeke snapped. "This was *Cece* once, all right. Don't act like you were any better, Cross."

"Yeah. Fair enough."

"Move away from the door," Catherine murmured quickly, "before they catch you there, Roz."

She did, and took a tart from Catherine's outstretched hand in just enough time to make the two men think she hadn't been listening to their conversation at all. Catherine didn't say a word differently, either.

Roz was still left with questions.

*Way too many questions.*

# FOURTEEN

Naz tugged the beanie down over his ears as he hung the helmet to his bike up on the steering wheel. "Didn't know you were going to be over this way today, Luca."

His best friend tipped his chin up from where he stood on the steps of his parents' home leaning against the railing. Dragging a hard inhale from the smoke, Luca eyed Naz in a way that set him on edge. Although, he wasn't really sure *why* it put him on edge. It just fucking did.

Naz stepped off the bike, and cocked a brow. "Something wrong?"

"You tell me, man."

Naz stiffened.

Yeah, definitely something wrong.

Luca took another drag from his cigarette and watched the cherry red tip flicker and then explode across the asphalt of the driveway when he flicked it from his fingertips. "Didn't know *you* were coming this way tonight, either."

"I called you this morning—told you I caught a flight instead of driving back. What the fuck is wrong with you? Speak up if you've got something to say, but I've got better things to do than deal with your shitty mood that I don't even understand."

Sure, Luca was his best friend, but that didn't mean Naz was going to take *any* kind of shit from the man because he wouldn't. He never had. Oh, they had gone through their rounds over the years. Nothing too serious, though. A couple of busted mouths, and black eyes. Stupid teenage shit that pitted the two friends against each other for whatever reason, and sent their fists flying.

They worked it out.

They always did.

Luca chuckled as he nodded, and stepped down from the stairs. Stuffing his hands in his pockets, the younger man glanced up at the sky. It wasn't nightfall yet, but they were in twilight. That time of day when the sun wasn't quite peeking over the horizon, but it was still light enough to be comfortable and nice.

Naz's favorite time of the day.

And right then, he really just wanted to spend it with Rosalynn. He'd been gone all fucking week with no phone on him except a burner he couldn't use to call anyone but his partner, the buyer, and his father if something went wrong. *That* was the rule for gunrunning. The less communication on a run, the better. And if one of them did happen to get caught while on the run, the phone that was confiscated could only lead back to one or two people. Nothing that would do very much at the end of the day.

It was all quite purposeful.

Usually, he'd come home from a week-long run and go straight to his mother and father's. That way, he could fill Cross in on any details his father needed to know, have dinner with his parents, and get back to work as usual the next day as a man trying to get his button for Cosa Nostra.

That was Naz's whole life in a nutshell.

Not lately, though.

Lately, it was all about Roz.

The fucking guns just got in the way for a bit.

But not now because Naz was back, and he didn't have a gun run for another few months, at least. There would be nothing—other than the usual day to day work shit—keeping him away from Roz.

Naz moved forward, taking his steps carefully even as Luca came toward him, too. The two friends met in the middle of the driveway. Luca still looked like he was some kind of pissed off, and ready to rip Naz's throat apart with his bare hands.

It was the *why* Naz didn't get.

"Seriously, just spit it the fuck out," Naz told his friend. "Is it Roz? Because I'm messing with her, or …?"

Luca let out a bitter laugh. "Yes, and *no*."

"That makes no fucking—"

"You didn't even tell her where you were going, Naz," Luca snapped, his blue eyes turning on his friend with a fire blazing behind them. "You just fucking *took off* on her without even a goddamn note."

"Hey, I said I had business to do."

Luca scoffed. "*Business.* Do you know what that shit means to my sister? It means going into the city for a couple of days like Dad does, Naz. She's not fucking stupid—she knows what he is, and what *your* father is. She probably knows what you are. She doesn't know the finer details, though."

"She also hasn't *asked*, Luca."

"So, then you fucking tell her anyway." Luca shrugged. "What you don't do is spend *day after day* with her, and then drop off her radar like it's nothing. That fucks with her head, even if you don't mean for it to. And you know what, if you fuck with my sister's head again, I'll fucking beat your ass. Got it?"

Naz blinked, his hackles clanging. That cocky part of him that didn't know how to let a threat go unanswered thought to rise right to the fucking occasion, even if it was his friend who threatened him ... and even if Luca was kind of justified at the moment.

"Excuse me?" Naz asked, moving closer to his friend again.

Luca moved forward, too. "You heard what I said, Naz."

The two men were so close that if Naz or Luca leaned in, their fucking foreheads would touch. He had a crystal clear view of the anger and challenge in Luca's gaze. There was no doubt his friend wasn't fucking around today.

The fucking arrogant idiot Naz was meant he didn't see those things as warnings he should heed, but rather, something he wanted to face head on. See just how far he could push Luca because why the hell not?

"*My* business," Naz drawled out slowly, "isn't any of your fucking business. Do you got *that*?"

"My sister—"

"Stay the fuck out of my business, Luca."

Luca's gaze flashed, and Naz didn't even see that fucking fist coming from his friend until it was too late. He wouldn't call it a cheap shot, necessarily. He'd pushed his friend's line, and Luca decided to answer that call with his own actions.

Fair was fucking *fair*, after all.

Naz always said so.

Nonetheless, that punch landed hard against Naz's jaw, and sent his head spinning to the side. He might have felt a tooth or two come loose, too, but it was hard to say. He was a little distracted by the pain stinging through the side of his face, and the blood blooming across his tongue.

*Fuck.*

Naz laughed, and shook his head as he spat the blood to the ground and righted himself. Luca had moved back a step, and had his hands resting down by his side. Other than the clenching of the fist that he'd hit Naz with, and the reddening of his knuckles, one wouldn't be able to tell that the man had hit him at all. All Luca's anger was gone, and he seemed done with the entire show.

Nodding, Naz murmured, "You put some fucking weight behind that one."

Luca shrugged. "It'll only hurt for a while, asshole."

"Yeah, I bet."

Naz ran his tongue along his inner cheek to rid the rest of the blood, and eyed his friend all the while. "I know it's your fucking sister, but you know I'm not here to mess around with her in that kind of way, either. It's not like that, so back off."

"Then, don't make her feel like that and this won't have to happen again. Are we clear, or what?"

Yeah, he got it.

"My bad," Naz murmured.

Luca cleared his throat, and stuffed his hands in his pockets as he inched forward to come closer to Naz once more. "And I guess, I'm sorry about the whole hitting you thing even if you did deserve it for acting like a prick. Because you *are.*"

"Someone's gotta keep me in line."

His friend laughed, still coming closer. "Right?"

Pulling one hand out of his pocket, Luca moved to offer it to Naz to shake. Their way of saying let bygones be bygones about the whole thing. It was their thing. It happened, and now it was fucking over.

Naz shook his friend's hand.

"If you're all quite done measuring dicks out here," came the sweetest voice Naz had ever heard in his life, "then I would like a second."

Naz grinned over Luca's shoulder, even as his friend sighed and rolled his eyes. "Hey, you."

Roz smiled even if it was faint. "Hey."

Luca clapped Naz on the shoulder, and moved toward his waiting Camaro. "Tomorrow for work, then?"

"Tomorrow, man. Same as usual."

"Let's hope you don't bruise."

"Fuck you."

Luca only laughed before slapping Naz on the cheek, and going on his way. Naz waited until his friend had pulled out of the drive, and was gone down the street before he turned back to face Roz again. She was still standing on the porch, and had her arms folded over her chest.

Now, this was where it became fucking *funny.*

Why?

Because he hadn't been the slightest bit afraid of his friend's anger when he first showed up, but he was fucking *terrified* of the way Roz looked in that moment.

Disappointed, and confused.

"I should have explained more before I took off," he said quietly, moving toward her. She said nothing, and as he came to the bottom steps, Naz added, "Gave you a clearer picture of where I was going to be, and why I couldn't call. I'm sorry I left you hanging all week."

Roz chewed on her inner cheek before asking, "Are you going to explain now?"

"Do you want me to?"

Because if she did, then he would.

It was that simple.

Roz nodded. "I think I do. I know you're … I know you do *family* business, Naz. I know that, okay. You don't have to keep me in the dark."

Naz smirked, and climbed the stairs until he was standing right in front of this beautiful, crazy girl who just because he could, he loved inexplicably. It was strange and scary and entirely wonderful.

"It's more than family business, Roz," he said quietly.

She looked up at him, although she didn't have to stare very far to meet his gaze. "Oh?"

"Way more."

"And sometimes that means you drop off the radar for a while, I take it."

"Safety reasons," he said, chuckling "Call it good fucking policy, yeah?"

"And how often—"

"Few times a year."

Roz glanced away. "For what?"

"Guns. People buy them. I run them to the buyer."

He didn't miss the stiffening of her shoulders, or the way a knot formed between her brows like she was trying to figure that out.

"So, what does all that mean, Naz?"

"I guess that I'm far more than just a genius, Roz."

A bad man who did bad things.

Sinful.

Criminal.

And yet, he was none of those things when he was with her.

Not at all.

"Sorry if that's all you were looking for with me," he added after a moment.

Roz's gaze turned back on him in a blink.

All fire.

Life.

And *love*.

"I was looking for you," she whispered. "I'm looking at *you*."

Naz closed that distance between them in a heartbeat, and crashed his lips down on hers in a bruising kiss.

It'd been too long, anyway.

A week without kissing this woman was way too long.

# FIFTEEN

Roz could feel his gaze on her. From where in the room, she didn't know. It was hard to tell when it seemed like her parents had invited every person they knew to Luca's birthday party. Oh, she loved her parents for the fact they always celebrated their children's birthdays even now that Luca and Roz were probably beyond the age of all that.

Still, she wondered where Naz was.

She could feel his gaze on only her. It was the way her skin hummed with the strangest buzzing sensation. Like all the fine hairs lifted from the back of her neck, and her breaths came out a little shorter than normal. She *loved* that feeling, and yet ... she still wished she could watch him, too.

She couldn't see him, though.

Her gaze scanned the crowd even as her hands continued moving over familiar keys on the piano. She didn't need to actually look down to know what she was doing when it came to the piano. Especially not if it was a composition she was very familiar with and had been playing for years.

She wasn't actually supposed to play the piano tonight for the guests, anyway, but someone thought it would be a great idea. Roz got roped into it because she didn't like telling people no, and her parents *loved* showing off her hard work.

Some things never changed ...

Roz didn't break stride or form as she looked for Naz in the crowd. Her smile was still firmly in place as her gaze drifted over the faces of familiar people. Back straight, shoulders loose but firm, and arms at the correct position for her hands to do all the work. She was sure everyone just thought she was smiling for them, but really, she wanted to find *him*.

He'd been back for a few days—things went back to normal. Just like he said. Like he hadn't been gone at all.

If anything, that only made Roz edgier. For reasons she wasn't even sure of, to be honest. Like she might blink, and he'd be gone again.

Even if he promised that wasn't the case.

That fear hung on.

Soon enough, Roz had finished the piece on the piano and was standing from the bench before the clapping had even started. The guests did clap, though. The noise was thunderous. She heard the congratulations and praise, and took them all with a smile. Even the arms reaching to hug her, and pat her cheeks as people told her how much she had grown up since the last time they saw her.

People kept saying that.

She didn't see it like they did.

Moving through the last few people while accepting their hugs, too, Roz finally spotted Naz. *Finally*.

She was entirely unsurprised to find he had tucked himself into the far corner of the room where he couldn't be bothered. She found he didn't like that very much. *Hated* when people interrupted him while he was watching her.

He looked like a woman's walking wet dream standing there in a three-piece suit, his hair pulled back like he'd been dragging his fingers through the strands, and a glass of whiskey in his hands. Easy posture, lazy smile, and eyes only on her. He looked like he didn't have a fuck to give in the world because he had everything he wanted standing just a few feet away from him right then.

Naz grinned, and winked.

Roz smiled back.

Soon enough, she was going to hide that grin of his when her lips found his. She *swore* ... would put her hand on a fucking bible to say it ... that her music was made better when this man was watching her. Something about him being there made her hyperaware, and the music just sounded better.

It didn't have to be reasonable.

It just was.

"That was beautiful, Roz."

Katya slipped in beside her daughter, and took her attention away from Naz for a moment. As much as it *sucked*, she supposed she could wait another few seconds before she could get back to where she wanted to be.

Tucked right into his side.

With him.

"Thanks, Ma," Roz said.

Her mother looked at someone over Roz's shoulder before her gaze came back to her daughter. "When you're playing sounds like that, it makes me wonder why you're still considering backing out of that audition."

Roz sucked in a sharp breath.

Here?

*Really?*

Her mother wanted to bring that up *right now?* It was not the right time at all. It was not another argument Roz wanted to have, either. She'd been arguing with her parents about this all damn week.

Couldn't they let it rest?

Wasn't it bad enough that they had gone behind her back to tell her mentor what she was considering without letting her have enough time to figure it out on her own?

Apparently, no.

That had not been a fun conversation.

"We talked about this," Roz reminded her mother.

Katya nodded. "And I still think you're making a mistake. It's not that you're not ready, Rosalynn. It's that your mind is *elsewhere*."

"So?"

Her mother blinked. "I beg your pardon?"

"So," Roz snapped again, although she kept her voice at a reasonable level so that they didn't draw attention from the guests. There was no need to go ruining her brother's birthday party, even if he hadn't asked for this party. "So what if that's what it is, Ma. So what if I'm distracted, and now is not the right time?"

"Because spots in that company only come up once in a decade, and if you're *very* lucky, you might get two chances in a decade. That's why."

Nothing Katya said was a lie.

Roz just didn't need the fucking reminder.

"I don't feel ready," Roz told her mother. "And there's nothing I can do about that except hold off on the audition. I would rather hold off than go when I'm not ready, Ma."

Katya sipped from the wine in her hand, and sighed. "Your father thinks maybe you should go back to—"

"No."

"And what if you don't go to the audition, then what?"

"I don't understand."

"What do you plan to do? You'll get your official diploma next week, and have the ceremony next month. *If* you even choose to go to that, mind you. But what about after? What are your plans?"

Roz's shoulders stiffened at the tone of her mother's voice. "Maybe I'll stay in New York. Would that be such a bad thing?"

"It might be," her mother replied, "if there's only *one* reason you're doing that for."

"You mean to say one person, Ma."

"You're seventeen."

"Eighteen next month," she shot back fast.

Katya smiled. "That doesn't negate the fact that you're still young, *dushka*. Young, and prone to making rash decisions. I don't want you to give up on your dreams. And if you asked that *one person*, I bet he would say the same thing. Wouldn't he? If he cared, and he means to you what you think he does … wouldn't he say the same thing, Rosalynn? Have you even asked?"

Roz found Naz was still staring at her when she glanced to the side. He grinned in that way of his again. The way that had her heart pounding, and her stomach doing the strangest flip-flops. All he had to do was fucking stare at her, and her whole world suddenly felt like it had flipped on its axis, and nothing was ever going to be the same again.

That was the thing.

She was here now.

He was hers.

Nothing could be the same.

She didn't want it to be, either.

Katya sighed, and drew Roz's attention back to her mother. "I see."

"What?"

"You haven't asked him, have you? I bet you haven't mentioned to him at all that you're considering scrapping the audition, and instead of continuing your career, you plan to stay here in New York. Because this is where he is. You haven't told him any of those things at all."

No, she hadn't.

Because what did it matter?

"It's still *my* choice, Ma," Roz said.

"It is," her mother agreed, "but what if it's the wrong choice?"

"That's for me to figure out, too."

Katya smiled softly. "It is, you're right. I still think you should ask him, though, and explain. He might surprise you. You know ..."

"What?"

She tried to keep the irritation out of her tone, but it was impossible. Her mother acted like Roz was cool, calm, and relaxed. That was Katya— she could handle anything. Roz wished she could say the same.

"You're allowed to be in love, and still have your own dreams, Roz. All those dreams don't have to only be for him."

Was that how it worked?

Right now, it certainly didn't feel like it.

Before Roz could respond to her mother, someone dragged Katya away to talk to someone else. Roz didn't even get the chance to slip through the last bit of the crowd in the room to get back to Naz. Someone dragged her away, too.

Someone else to tell her just how much she'd *grown up*.

They had no fucking idea.

# SIXTEEN

Naz, at best, was an impatient fucker. It could be considered his greatest flaw if he cared to think about his few flaws. Except he didn't … and he was more than willing to embrace all his impatientness when it came right down to it.

Throwing back the last bit of whiskey—he'd let himself have *one* glass for this party just in case Roz wanted to get the hell out of there later and he had to drive—he peered over the crowd again to see if he could find his girl. He swore every time he laid eyes on her, someone else was coming around to take her away.

He hadn't gotten five minutes of conversation with her the whole night. It was driving him *nuts*.

A hand clapped his shoulder hard on the left side, and Naz relaxed a bit at the sound of his father's quiet chuckles. "What are you doing over here in the corner, Naz?"

"Maybe I'm letting Luca have his spotlight."

Cross arched a brow like he was considering that statement. "I *might* believe that, if you actually thought you might take it away. You wouldn't—you're not the type. Try again."

His gaze swept the crowd again. "Did you see where Roz went?"

"Ah."

He would not look over at his father. He *would not*.

Except he did.

Cross was wearing a shit-eating smirk again. *Goddammit.* "Everyone taking up her attention and time, and I bet you're a sad little puppy over here."

Just the tone of his father's voice was enough to make Naz bristle. "I swear, if you try to pet my head like—"

His father slapped his cheek twice instead. "Nope, just going to enjoy pestering the fuck out of you, son. No one else dares to."

That was mostly true.

Luca did, sometimes.

"You know, back when I was your age and this was me and Catherine … I used to just sneak her out the first chance I could. We'd take off, and it'd be hours later before someone realized we were even gone. *Good times.*"

Usually, when his father talked about *things* like that regarding his mother, Naz tuned him out. He didn't need to know those things of things. But that was actually kind of helpful, and he was going to *pull a Cross* as his mother liked to say.

He was his father's twin, after all.

Or that's what everyone told him his whole fucking life.

Naz's lips split with a sly smile. "That sounds like a great idea."

"Hey, I didn't—"

"Thanks, Papa."

He heard his father's sigh echo behind him as he turned his back to his father, and headed into the crowd. If he couldn't find Roz, then she could come and find him. And once she did, they'd be gone.

Perfect, really.

"There you are," Roz said as she slipped out the front door of her parents' home. Her wide smile made Naz grin, too. "I've been looking for you."

"I bet."

"What's that supposed to mean?"

Naz chuckled, and shook his head. "Means nothing. I just figured instead of waiting for you to find me in there, it might be better if you found me out here."

Roz eyed him curiously as she came down the steps. The chill in the air wasn't too bad, but it was enough that he could see a slight shiver crawling over her exposed shoulders under the dress she wore. Once she was close enough for him to reach out and grab her, Naz did just that.

Her laughter colored up the driveway—filled to the brim with cars from guests—as Naz dragged her into his warm chest. He used his jacket to wrap around her as she tucked her arms in close to his body. Resting her chin on his pec, she peered up at him with a brilliant smile curving her sweet lips.

"Better?" he asked.

"Is what better?"

"You were cold."

Roz's gaze softened. "Yeah, it's better, Naz."

"Good."

He tightened his hold around her, refusing to let go. Now that he had her outside of that house, there was no way he was letting her go back in so someone else could steal her away from him again.

Nope.

Wasn't happening.

"Do you wanna get out of here?" he asked.

Roz laughed. "Oh, my *God*."

"What?"

"More than you know. I swear they invite *everybody*, and then the house is so fucking full of people you can't breathe. It happens every time, so you know they never learn."

Naz shrugged. "Gotta let them have their fun. Everybody enjoyed seeing you play, though, didn't they?"

He didn't miss the way she stiffened in his arms, but she kept her smile firmly in place anyway. "Yeah, seems so."

"What's that about?"

"Hmm?"

"You went still just now. I mentioned the piano, and you went—"

Roz shook her head. "Nothing. It's nothing."

No, it was definitely something. Tonight wasn't the night he wanted to have his first battle with Roz, though, so if she didn't want to talk about whatever it was, he'd let it go. But not for long. Just for *now*. She'd figure it out that he wasn't the kind of man who forgot *anything* when the right time came.

Naz would make sure of it.

Back to the better issue at hand …

"But you know, people are pouring alcohol now," he said, "so I don't think they'd even notice us gone."

Roz arched a brow high as she looked up at him again. "Is that why you came out here? You had this all planned, did you? Figured instead of trying to find me in all the people, you'd let *me* do the work to find you. And then we'd sneak out of here to go have some real fun. That's it, huh?"

He tried to look innocent.

And failed like a fucker.

"No," he said slyly.

Roz just laughed, and patted a hand against his chest. "I don't even care. Did you have something in mind? Where are we going?"

"Wherever you want, babe. It's always about what you want, Roz."

Didn't she know that?

She should.

"Let's go to your place," she said suddenly, pushing away from him and heading for where he'd parked his car—not the bike this time—at the very end of the driveway. Naz knew better than to try and get a closer spot to the house. No one could ever leave when their vehicle was crowded by everyone else's. "We can go there, right?"

He was still watching her walk away. "Is that where you want to go? There's not much to see at my place. We can go anywhere, Roz."

"Why not?"

Yeah ... why not?

"So, what do you think?" Naz asked.

Roz leaned in his bedroom doorway, and peeked at the space in there. He wasn't a big decorator, and he didn't plan on living here forever, so he hadn't put in much effort other than furniture, and a few things on the wall. The only thing that really meant anything to him inside the apartment was the Baby Grand piano in the living room that his grandfather, Calisto, had passed onto him when he first moved into the place. He certainly wasn't at Roz's level of talent when it came to the piano, but he knew a song or two and the scales.

Good enough for him.

"It's cute," she said.

Naz scoffed. "*Cute?*"

She shot him a sweet smile over her shoulder. "It feels very much like a bachelor lives here."

His lips split with a smirk. "I'm not *really* a bachelor now, though, am I? I have *you*."

Roz winked as she spun in the bedroom doorway. "Yeah, you still are even with me."

"Ah, I see."

"What is that above your bed, anyway?"

Naz didn't even have to look in the bedroom to know what she was talking about. The equation above his bed had been left unfinished, and the large six-foot by three-foot whiteboard was only half filled with numbers and symbols. Ready for him to get back to it whenever he felt the need.

"Time," he said. "It's time."

"Above your bed?"

Naz shrugged. "I've always had a whiteboard above my bed. I do my best thinking first thing in the morning, or right before I go to sleep. I need it close to translate what's in my head as it comes to me."

"And what's on that board—"

"Is an equation—or the formula for an equation—about time, yeah."

Roz peeked back over her shoulder. "How so?"

"It's an equation for the idea that *if* time was on a constant loop, one that doesn't end, then it would be more like an oval shape instead of the traditional infinity symbol most people think of when we think about infinite time."

"Why?"

He chuckled, and shoved his hands in his pockets. Why she wanted to know, he didn't understand. It was just a boring theory in his head that hadn't left him alone from the time he was sixteen. He'd finally decided to put it to paper even if he had dropped out of college, and left physics behind.

"Because with the idea of it being the traditional shape, at some point, time has to *meet* again. There's a point where it crosses over, and we know by the fact no one has ever recorded it happening ... time has never crossed over again. Instead, like an oval, we have long stretches of time that seem to mirror past events. They aren't exactly the same, but they feel very similar. People have moments of—"

"Deja vu," Roz interjected, smiling a little.

"Yeah, like that. So, I just thought if I could work out the math for this theory, then maybe it would be a new way to look at it."

"And that's all you plan to do with it? Just work out the math, and *look at it?*"

Naz's tongue peeked out to touch his upper lip as he laughed. "Yeah, babe. Sometimes my head is full of so much shit that I just ... have to get it out somehow. And that's one way I do it."

Roz stepped out of the bedroom doorway, and closer to him. "Is it always like that—your mind, I mean? Just *overflowing* and too much all the time?"

He stilled when her hand came up to brush against his jaw, and then her fingertips danced over his temple softly.

"Not when I'm with you," he murmured. "It's ... quiet when I'm with you."

Which was exactly why he hadn't been able to get back to that equation. Why he hadn't been able to finish it despite having it banging around in his head like a wasp that wouldn't leave him alone for years.

*Finally,* he found the one thing in the world that made all this crazy shit in his head go quiet. And she was fucking perfect.

Absolutely perfect.

"I forgot for a moment," Roz whispered.

Naz smiled as she inched closer until their noses were touching, and her lips grazed his as she spoke.

"Forgot what, Roz?"

"How smart you are. It's just … I forgot because you're pretty amazing in every other way, too. The genius thing is just something else to add to it, I guess."

"I'm not amazing," Naz said. "I'm just me."

"Maybe."

He heard her unspoken words.

But not to her.

He was amazing to her.

"Naz?"

Hmm?"

She was still watching him in that way—like she was seeing him for the first time all over again, and nothing else mattered.

"You know I didn't come here just to look around your place and talk, right?"

Naz kissed her softly. "Yeah, I know. But it's all on you, girl. Whatever you want, whenever you want it. I love you, so it's always on you."

Roz's blue eyes darkened. "Do you really?"

"What?"

"Love me that much."

So very much.

His hands came up to cup her throat and jaw, so he could keep her looking at only him. "Let me show you, Roz. Can I show you how I love you?"

His lips were on hers again when she whispered, "Please."

# SEVENTEEN

Roz was acutely aware of cool air whispering over her skin the very same way Naz's mouth followed the same path. Her skin prickled with goosebumps every single time his lips touched down in a new place. Her bare shoulder, the column of her throat, and then her chin. His tongue would strike out to taste her, too, with each kiss.

It was slow.

*Soft.*

Deliberate.

It had to be deliberate. Because with each touch of his hands sliding along her curves and removing clothing, and every kiss finding new places on her skin to taste ... the heat pooling in her gut intensified. It sent warmth shooting down between her thighs, and it made her shake.

*So breathless.*

She was so caught up in the way he was taking his time to learn her body that she barely realized she was now standing in nothing but a light blue lace bralette and panty set. That he'd somehow removed all of her clothes, and mostly his, too. So fucking distracted by him, in fact, that she didn't know they were inside his bedroom until the backs of her legs hit the bed.

*Oh, my God.*

"Naz," he murmured against the hollow of her throat. "Not *God*. Naz, babe. And you can say it as loudly and as often as you want tonight."

Roz blinked.

Had she said that out loud?

*Damn.*

And then his lips left her throat but only so that he could get her mouth crushed against his instead. Roz barely even felt the softness of the sheets grazing her legs as she was pushed down against the mattress. It was easy to forget where she was when all she wanted was him, and *more*.

Too easy, really.

His rough palms soothed her shaking thighs with warm strokes. Up, and then down. Up, and then *inward*. Roz found widening her legs to let him slip in between was second nature. No hesitancy, and no fear.

She thought she would be nervous.

Shouldn't she be?

It was easy with Naz.

Like *breathing*.

She expected him to lower to the bed with her, but instead, he went to his knees. Roz sucked in a sharp breath when his mouth ghosted over her navel, and then lower still. His knuckles grazed her inner thighs and sent shivers racing over her skin.

It was only him moving between her thighs from his position kneeling on the floor that sent her racing out of that daze he'd put her in. No one had ever, ever, *ever* done what she thought he was going to do. And that was enough to make her nervous.

"Wait, what—"

"Shh," Naz murmured, "there's a hell of a lot more to fucking than *fucking*, Roz. You see, if I just wanted to *fuck*, it's not going to be good for you at all. At least, not this time around. It'll be too fucking much, and it'll hurt. You don't want that, and neither do I. Right?"

She sucked in a sharp breath when those knuckles of his slid over the line of her panties, and sent shocks jolting through her nerves. "Right."

His dark gaze lifted to find hers and he echoed, "Right, babe. So, I'm going to make you feel amazing first. Get you feeling *high*. Because this here …" Two of his fingers slipped under the gusset of her panties, and slid along her center. Soft strokes of his fingers against her clit had her lips falling open, and noises crawling out of her that she hadn't heard before. "Yeah, this here needs *loved*, and I'm going to enjoy doing that. It needs to be ready, Roz. And then it's only going to feel really fucking good. Okay?"

Roz wasn't even sure how the word slipped past her lips given the fact she felt like she couldn't take in air, but it still did. "Okay."

"That's what I wanna hear." Naz leaned in, and that teasing mouth of his edged around her center while his fingers *played*. Those fucking fingers of his were working her into another daze, only this one was sure to end beautifully. "And I want to hear you, Roz. You make the best music with your fingers, but I bet what comes out of your mouth is going to be something else entirely. And I want to *hear it*."

*Fuck.*

His fingers came out of her long enough to pull the panties down her thighs, and then they were right back where she wanted them to be. Along with his mouth, too.

Roz hadn't been expecting it to feel like *that*.

Like his mouth was touching every single part of her all at the same time, except it was really only on *one* part of her. His fingers teased, and his mouth stroked. Tasting, and driving her higher and higher.

"*Please*," Roz breathed.

Her shoulders hit the bed, and her back arched high. Fingers tangling into his hair because she needed *something* to hold onto. She knew what was coming, that orgasm … but it'd never quite felt like that before.

Never so sudden.

Never so strong.

Never so … *everywhere*.

And when she did finally fall from that high, high place … she wasn't sure what she had expected. Certainly not for Naz to climb up over her with his legs pinning her to the bed as his hand circled her jaw, and he tilted her head back before his lips came down on hers. All the while, his hand was still working between her thighs. Harder, and faster. Pressing into a spot that had her shaking and whining even as he kissed her with the taste of her sex still on his mouth.

Maybe *that* was what made her come again.

Her taste on him.

The wildness in his eyes.

His hand holding her down.

Soft, and harsh, and *way too much*.

It still wasn't nearly enough.

He had been right, though. More than, even. Once she had finally stopped trembling like a little leaf in the hurricane that was him, she was so fucking ready. It ached between her thighs, but not because she was hurting. Because she needed more. Something else entirely.

So fucking wet, her thighs were slick.

*Crazy*.

That's how she felt.

Crazy.

So much so, that she pushed him back to the bed, and straddled him. Under the thin cotton of his boxer-briefs, the hard ridge of his erection pressed against her center when he reached for her again. Soft hands, but a tight hold.

He handled her like she was precious.

Careful, but *firm*.

His mouth was against hers again, whispering and promising. "It's all on you, babe. It's all you."

It took but a minute for Naz to find a condom in the bedside table, and slide it down his length after pushing his boxer-briefs down before he was back where she wanted him the most. It was only once she had him in her hands, and pressing between her thighs that she finally felt like she could breathe again. There was no pain when she lowered down on him, only an overwhelming sense of fullness as she was filled in a whole new way.

It took a second.

And then *two*.

His hands on her face, and his mouth on hers. A shuddering exhale dancing across her cheek when he was all there, and she just needed a minute.

She was never going to get this moment back. This one perfect moment. It would never be exactly like this again even if it did only get better.

So, she wanted to feel it.

*Remember* it.

Naz's thumb drew a line down Roz's trembling lips. His gaze drifted over her face, slow and *knowing*. "Fucking look at you, huh?"

"I don't know what to—"

"*Move,*" he murmured. "Don't fucking ever worry about *me*. It's about you, babe."

Roz watched him through lowered lashes. The clench of his teeth when she shifted her hips, and the way his sounds deepened when she grinded against him. He might not have wanted her to worry about him, but her view was so much better when she did.

This was how she learned.

By *sight*.

And she liked what she was looking at.

She loved it.

"You make me crazy," she told him.

"I know."

# EIGHTEEN

"I'm sorry, what?" Cross asked. "I'm going to need you to tell me that again, Nazio."

Naz stared up at the ceiling and wished it would swallow him whole. He was not the type to make these kinds of fuck-ups, but here he was. And his father was in no way going to let him get away with it like it hadn't happened at all. Cross just wasn't the type, and frankly, he knew his son only really learned from his mistakes when he was forced to face them head-on.

This wasn't quite the same.

He knew why he screwed up, and it wasn't going to happen again. He really didn't need his screw-ups pointed out in front of a bunch of other people, but here they were.

"*Why* did you miss grabbing those racket payments for the Capos?" his father asked. "And the bookie on the west side, too? Why?"

"Busy," Naz said, offering nothing else.

Quiet murmurings colored the restaurant behind Naz. It wasn't often he was invited to tribute because, at the moment, he wasn't a made man. That was the entire purpose of tribute. It wasn't for every man. It was only for the boss, and his men.

Naz was there because he fucked up for two different Capos in one week. It didn't matter that he had corrected those errors quickly. The fact remained the same, he'd still done something wrong.

"Naz," his father said quietly. "Look at me, huh?"

His gaze drifted to his father. It had been far easier to just stare at the wall of the restaurant while Cross scolded him than to look at his father directly. He didn't find anger in his father's stare—not that he expected to; Cross wasn't the type to get angry with his son—but he did find confusion and concern staring back at him.

Maybe a little disappointment.

Shit.

That was just as bad as anger.

If not worse.

"I fucked up," Naz said, "but I fixed it. It won't happen again."

"I don't doubt that," Cross returned, "but that isn't what I asked. I asked *why*. You haven't given me a proper answer yet, Naz."

He sighed. "I would rather not—"

"I didn't ask what you would rather do. I asked what I asked because I said what I *said*, Nazio. And you're going to give me an answer because that's what you do when your boss demands one."

Yeah, *fuck*.

Because right now, he was not dealing with his father at all. He was dealing with the Donati boss. A Cosa Nostra Don. It was a delicate line to balance, he thought. He really didn't know how his father managed it, but Cross *did*. And he did it well. Plus, it wasn't often his father had to pull rank on him anyway. Nazio was a good little soldier for *famiglia*. He knew what he had to do, when to do it, how to fucking do it, and not to ask questions.

He was just ...

"I got a little sidetracked," he muttered.

He was entirely off his game, more like it.

Cross straightened in his chair, and his gaze drifted to the men who were still eating and chatting behind him. Despite the fact their conversation was low, that didn't mean anything. They were having this conversation here for a purpose. Because those men could hear the conversation, and Cross wanted them to. He *wanted* his men to know he handled issues when they came up, even if it was his own son who caused the problem.

No doubt, his father couldn't afford for anyone to think he let shit slide. Not even if it was Nazio who made the shit fucking happen.

It bothered Naz, but not for reasons people probably expected. For one, he hated that he put his father in this position at all. He knew better than to be doing nonsense like this. And for two, because he *wasn't* a fuck up. A lot of these men had watched him grow up, and he spent a good portion of his childhood in this very restaurant with his father every single tribute.

Why?

Because he was the *principe*.

The Donati prince.

He knew better.

And he hated this just as much as his father did.

Cross likely knew it, too.

Not that it would change this whole meeting, or what his father had to do because of Nazio's mistakes. It wouldn't. Nazio couldn't be treated any differently than any other man trying to get his button for the family. He certainly had the privilege of being the son of a boss, but that didn't extend him very many special allowances at the end of the day.

And Naz didn't want it to.

"But *why?*" his father asked again. "Why the distraction? What happened? This isn't like you at all."

Roz.

Or … mostly her.

Two weeks had been spent with him trying to get as much time with her as he could. In his bed, and out of it. She was like a hungry little kitten. All claws, and softness waiting for him day after day. It was fucking *addictive*. Naz hadn't really considered some of the shit he was letting fall to the wayside because his brain wasn't the type to fail him in that kind of way. He kept up on *everything*. Distracted or not.

Apparently, not this time.

"I got caught up in other things," he offered to his father instead of outing the name of the daughter of the man sitting right beside Cross. Zeke wouldn't appreciate that, and frankly, Naz hadn't even had a decent conversation with the man since he started dating Zeke's daughter. He figured today was not the day Zeke wanted to hear this kind of shit, or have that conversation. It was the respect of the matter. "I'll make sure it doesn't happen again, boss."

Cross's jaw tightened. A sure sign his father was irritated that he wasn't getting the answers he wanted from his son. But that was the thing about Naz, and his father knew it all too well.

Twins, right?

They were too alike for their own good.

Naz was stubborn as fuck. A brick wall when it came right down to it. If he didn't want to say something, not even a gun to his temple was going to make those words come out. That's just how it worked for him.

His father was the same.

Cross cleared his throat, and straightened a bit in his seat. "Fine, then. Since you know you set us back a bit this week, then you won't mind picking up the slack for the other Capos' men who have helped *you* this week to correct your mistakes. You're to take on a duty from each of them, and handle it until the *wedding*, Nazio."

He blinked, and did the math in his head.

That was ten guys, at least.

And the wedding—his sister's—was a month and a half away.

Not impossible, as Naz could make anything work if he put his mind to it. Or rather, like in this case, he wasn't given much of a fucking choice. But that meant he was going to get a hell of a lot less time with Roz, and he really didn't know how to tell her that. None of this had been her fault. It was his screw up, and he should have remedied it before it got this far.

"Okay," Naz said.

Cross eyed his son for another few seconds like he was trying to figure something out before he flicked a hand. A silent dismissal if Naz had ever seen one. He knew better than to linger after his father did something like that.

Outside the restaurant, Naz found a comfortable spot leaning against the brick and patted the pockets of his jacket until he found what he wanted. It wasn't often that he smoked, but sometimes, shit just called for smoke and nicotine.

Today was one of those days.

He'd just lit up the cigarette and took a heavy drag when his father slid in beside him against the brick wall. For a time, Cross said nothing, and allowed Naz his silence and peace while he smoked. He was grateful.

It didn't last too long.

"You're distracted by her, aren't you?" his father asked. "That's what it is, and what you didn't want to say. Rosalynn."

Naz coughed, and took another drag from the smoke before shrugging. "Her father's sitting right there. What, you want me to discuss private matters about her in public with Zeke sitting right there, or …?"

"No, not particularly."

"There you go, then."

Cross shifted a bit in his stance so that his shoulder rested to the brick, and he was staring sideways at his son. "It's not like you to get overwhelmed with something, Naz."

"Quite aware, yeah."

"Tone down the attitude."

"What do you want me to say? I fixed what I messed up, and I'll handle the rest like you just told me to do. There's nothing else to say. It's done."

"Mmm," his father hummed noncommittally. "I know this is all new to you—*love*. And like everything that's new to you, and that fucking brain of yours, you need to throw yourself head first into it so that you know everything there possibly is to *know*. But here's a secret for you, Naz. Love isn't like everything else in life. You never stop learning with love, and that's part of the beauty of it."

He glanced over at his father, and wondered how Cross seemed to just know shit when it came to his son without needing to be told. Because fuck him for hitting the nail right on the head.

Cross continued on like Naz wasn't staring at him as though a second head had sprouted out of his neck. "The woman you fell in love with the first time isn't going to be the same woman when she's twenty-five, or thirty-two. She's going to change, and you're going to change. There will be more things to learn because that's what life does to you. So, I know this is hard for you to understand being your nature is just to absorb everything, and run with it … but you can't learn everything about love. It teaches you on its own time, Naz. You'll do well to figure that out. Find a balance. It's the only way you're going to make this work."

Well, then …

"I'm sorry," Naz muttered. "For screwing up."

Cross chuckled, and reached up to slap his son's cheek gently. "You're not even the hundredth man to fuck up, son. You're not going to be the last, either. It's okay to fail sometimes. I told you that once, didn't I? You don't have to be perfect, Nazio. Just because you're a goddamn genius doesn't mean you have to be the first at everything."

No, he just had to be him.

That's what his father always told him.

# NINETEEN

"Roz, could you come down here for a minute, please?"

Roz heard her mother's request, but she didn't really want to move. Maybe … *God*, maybe … if she stared at this damn piano long enough, her muse would come back. Her desire to make beautiful music would rush back, and consume her again.

So far, nothing.

"Roz!"

"Yeah," she called back, "I'm coming."

Roz checked her phone to find a couple of missed texts from Naz. Short texts that didn't tell her very much, honestly. He'd been so busy for a couple of weeks that she only got to see him for maybe an hour, and then he was gone again. It wasn't much, but it was better than nothing.

She supposed …

"Last ditch effort," she heard a familiar voice say. "We'll see if this can push her that last mile, right?"

Roz's brow knotted together as she headed toward that voice downstairs. There was no fucking way her mentor—

Sure enough, there Kyle stood in her parents' kitchen. Seemed he'd discarded his usual three-piece suits for khaki shorts, and a white T-shirt. She didn't think she had ever seen her mentor dress down before, but here he was doing exactly that.

Roz blinked. "Kyle."

The man smiled easily. "Roz."

In that moment, Roz wasn't sure whether to feel extremely pissed off that her parents had invited her mentor to their home without telling her, or grateful that they had done so. She was kind of pissed more than she was happy.

Hadn't she made herself clear?

"I'm not ready for the Australia audition," Roz said quietly. "And you being here isn't going to change that fact."

Kyle nodded, and passed her mother and father a look as he leaned against the island counter. "That's what I was told, yep. And you've said it more than enough times for me to hear it, Roz."

"Then, why are you—"

"Audition is in two weeks, and you're still on the docket."

Roz stiffened.

Kyle smiled like he didn't need her—or hell, maybe he didn't want her—to say anything in that moment. "You know *you* have to be the one who calls to request your spot be removed and filled with someone else. I couldn't do that for you. It had to be you. And here we are, two weeks out from the audition, and despite the fact you've said repeatedly that you're *not* going to go, you're still on the docket."

Fuck him for knowing that.

For having connections to get that information.

"So, I'll call tonight," Roz snapped. "What difference does it make?"

"Because you're not going to call, are you? You left your name on the docket because even though you don't feel ready, Roz, a part of you still wants to try. So, I'm here to make sure you at least give it your best shot."

Oh, that was rich.

*Really.*

"And what," Roz asked, "I get on that stage, and make a fool of myself because I'm not ready for it. I *fail* and then I don't get invited back when the next audition comes up? I lose my chance. I would rather not go at all."

Kyle tipped his head sideways a bit, and studied her. "You kept something from me, didn't you?"

Roz's gaze darted to her parents, and then back to her mentor. "No, I—"

"Mmm, yes. A young man, your parents said. *Nazio,* I believe his name is." Kyle cleared his throat, and waved a hand. "Could you two give us a few minutes, so I can speak with Rosalynn in private. I don't think this needs to be a public conversation."

Her parents didn't even need to be asked again. Despite the fact that Kyle had a good decade and a little more on her in years, when it came to her music, her parents *always* deferred to him to make the right choice. Roz didn't blame them at all. Since she had started to be mentored under Kyle, nothing about music was the same to her. It wasn't just about making a beautiful thing, but *living* within the beautiful thing she created. He made her a better pianist.

The best, maybe.

So why didn't she feel like it?

"The muse comes and goes, Roz," Kyle murmured when they were alone, "and sometimes, our muse changes when we don't expect it to. We look for the old muse expecting it to still be there, but it's changed. It's something new. *Someone* new. It can take us a while to figure it out because we creatives … well, we're a whole other breed of monsters, Roz. We don't like change, and when something in our comfortable medium changes, suddenly the whole world is coming to an end."

Her head snapped up, and she found her mentor was looking at her in that soft way of his. Like she was a little girl just learning how to walk, and he was going to help her every step of the way.

Kyle nodded. "And sometimes, our world coming to an end around us feels like being unable to play, or *think*. It could be wanting to do anything else but what we love the most. It can be a lot of things, and nothing at all at the same time. I wish you would have told me about the young man. I might have been able to explain this to you sooner, and we could have avoided these last couple of months, hmm?"

"Are you saying—"

"If your muse changed," Kyle said, "perhaps you just thought you lost it?"

"I'm not ready."

"You're ready. You're just scared."

She was.

She was terrified.

It was only partly about the fact she felt like she couldn't play. It was only a little bit about Naz, and how distracted she was lately. It was *a lot* about the fact she felt like a goddamn fake. It didn't matter how many beautiful melodies she created, or how many successes she'd already celebrated in her short, but amazing, career ... she was always going to feel like she wasn't good enough.

She was some seventeen-year-old *girl* from Nowhere, New York. She didn't have a whole pedigree of musical talent behind her name like some of the people she was expected to go up against, and despite training her whole life, it still didn't feel like enough.

She didn't *belong*.

"That," Kyle said, pointing at her face like he could read her mind. "*That right there,* Roz. I see it. We call that imposter syndrome. Creatives all over the world feel like this. People at the height of their success feel like this. And it's okay because it comes and goes, and it doesn't last forever. But you're not an imposter. You're just a girl sitting in front of a piano with a talent to share, and a stage being offered to allow you the chance to do that."

"I can't even focus long enough—"

"Then find what does make you focus," Kyle countered before she could even finish. "You find what does that, and you run with it, but you don't give in or give up. Are you going to take that chance, or let it go?"

*God.*

"I don't feel ready," she repeated again.

"That's an excuse, not a reason," Kyle countered. He drew out four slips of paper from his khakis pocket, and set them to the counter beside him. "Four plane tickets. Mine is online, and I don't need you to hold onto mine.

I didn't need to buy them—your parents have more than enough money to do that, but I still did. Do you want to know why?"

Roz shrugged.

What difference did it make?

"Because they love you enough to make you comfortable," he told her. "If you tell them no, they're going to listen. They're going to let you stay home, and wonder *what if* for the rest of your life. I wasn't put in your life to make you comfortable, or to give a single *fuck* about your reservations. I was put in front of you to make you work, and succeed."

*Jesus.*

"I was put here to challenge you because no one else is going to, Roz," Kyle said. "And if the audition is what breaks you, then I guess you weren't meant to do this, were you? But I don't think it will. *They* want to see you nail that audition. And so do I. *So, do it.*"

Roz's brow furrowed.

She and her parents made three.

"Who's the fourth one for, then?"

Kyle laughed. "Wouldn't *he* like to see you play, too? This … *Nazio*. I hear he's brilliant. Color me surprised that you went out and found someone like that. Is he brilliant enough to appreciate your brilliance, too? Or doesn't he know about the audition, Roz?"

She didn't speak.

She didn't have to.

Kyle nodded. "Where is your muse, Roz? It's always your muse that drives you. Follow the muse."

In her heart.

Her muse was in her heart.

*And in his.*

# TWENTY

"I can't play."

Naz blinked at the woman standing just beyond the front door of his apartment. "Roz?"

It wasn't that he was unhappy to see her there. Quite the fucking opposite, really. He missed her like nothing else. But he'd been so damn busy with handling his business, and the extra work put on his shoulders by his father for his fuckups that other than a call or text, he didn't get to see her much at all. An hour over the week to sit on her parents' porch, and watch the fucking sky, but that was *nothing*.

Nothing that he wanted to do, anyhow.

Roz looked him up and down like she was just seeing him standing there in nothing but boxer-briefs, and not as though she had been standing in his doorway for a whole minute staring at him. "Did you just get out of the shower?"

Naz dragged his fingertips through his wet hair to slick it back out of his eyes. "Yeah—came running when I heard the door. Shit's crazy, babe, so it could have been anybody with something for me to do."

Because that was his fucking life now.

Not that he wanted Roz to know it.

He really didn't want this girl thinking that just because he was too wrapped up in her to take care of other business that it was automatically her fault. It wasn't. None of it was her problem. This was all on him, and he needed to handle it one way or the other.

Like his father said … *find a balance.*

"I called you earlier," Roz added. "You didn't pick up."

Naz let out a slow breath. "I just got home, and went straight to the shower. My phone has been going off nonstop, and it might have gotten lost in the other shit. Sorry."

She frowned. "Oh."

"Hey, don't do that."

"No, you're … busy. Like you said. I don't want to bother—"

"*Roz.*"

Her head snapped up, and those beautiful, big blue eyes of her latched onto his gaze, and held strong. He refused to let her gaze drop, too, as he stepped forward with arms already open. She let him take her into his embrace, and he dropped a quick kiss to her forehead. Nothing felt better to him than having this woman in his arms, and it was strange as hell to him how that worked.

His whole life was one giant ball of stress right now. He couldn't fucking escape it if he tried. Not even a quarter of a bottle of whiskey before bed would do the trick, because fucking right, he'd even tried *that*.

But just having Roz there, and his arms around her ... shit was good again. His chaotic mind stopped the continuous chatter, and went silent. She was there, and that was all that mattered to him. It was no wonder that he had been so willing to just let shit slide in other points of his life when *this* wonder was what awaited him.

"You're not a bother," he promised. "And I was going to call you once I jumped out of the shower, anyway. I might have had a whole evening to myself if nobody calls, so I thought maybe you'd want me to spend it with you, huh?"

Roz nibbled on her bottom lip, and peered up at him. "Yeah?"

"Yep."

She smiled. "Okay."

But his evening wasn't really a guarantee, either. All it would take was a call from a Capo, or his father, or even Zeke ... and shit, there he would be, sent running somewhere again. It never ended, it seemed.

He also didn't have anyone to blame for that but himself, too. Naz was quite aware of that, so he didn't bother to complain. It wouldn't do him any good. He was going to handle his business like he should have done in the first place.

Naz didn't care about any of that right now though because he was a little concerned with the anxiety he found staring back at him from Roz. He wondered if that anxiousness had anything to do with her greeting—that wasn't really a greeting—when he'd first answered the door for her.

*I can't play.*

"What's wrong?" he asked.

She kept quiet, but Naz didn't need her words to confirm what he *felt*. In his heart, he just knew something was off.

"Everything," she finally whispered.

"Not us," he returned easily.

Roz smiled a bit. "No, and yes."

Naz didn't like that at all. "Come in, and give me a sec, yeah? Just gotta make a call."

She nodded, and he stepped aside to allow her into his apartment. Dropping another quick kiss to her forehead, Naz left Roz to take off her coat and shoes as he headed further into the apartment. He found his phone where he'd left it charging on the bedside table. A quick press of his finger against the screen, and the phone dialed a familiar number.

His father picked up on the second ring.

"Naz, what can I do for you?"

"Give me the night," Naz replied. "Call off any Capo that might need me, or send me running. I just … need one night."

"Can't do that, son. Sorry."

Naz let out a hard breath. "Listen, I wouldn't ask, but—"

"No, you know the rules, Nazio. Handle your business." Cross cursed under his breath, and then muttered, "Give me a minute—Zeke's calling."

He tried really fucking hard not to glare at the wall while the phone went silent, but it was *difficult*. He didn't ask his father for very much, but especially not when it came to the mafia. He knew he had to do this thing—get his button—on his own because if his father handed it to him, no one was ever going to respect him for that. But this wasn't the same thing, and he really just needed Cross to shut up and listen to him for once.

Okay, that was a little unfair. His father did listen to him, but Naz was aware Cross also had to act as his boss, and not just his dad, too. That couldn't be easy.

Naz told himself to remember that fact when his father came back on the line with a heavy sigh that echoed.

"Is Rosalynn with you tonight?" his father asked before he could say anything. "You know that was Zeke, and he was curious if I'd heard from you tonight because Roz took off. Apparently, her mentor came into town."

Naz blinked. "Doesn't he live in England where she goes to that school?"

"He does."

"Why would he come all the way—"

"Is she there?"

"She is. Just showed up. That's why I called. Something's … not right," he added quieter just in case Roz was somewhere near his bedroom and listening to his call. "With her, I mean. She seems off."

"I'm sure she does."

"What does that mean?"

"She's having a moment that's not my business to explain. Ask, son. And since *Zeke* thinks a night away might do her some good, but especially some time with you … you get your one night. Expect a call at five in the morning. Understood? Business as usual as of *five*, Nazio."

He blinked again.

Like a fucking idiot.

"What's going on?"

"Ask her. I hear she has a big audition coming up."

His father hung up the phone without letting Naz ask another question. He was left staring at his phone with more questions than he had answers, but he figured the girl wandering around in his apartment might be able to provide him with the information he needed.

Except ... Roz wasn't wandering his apartment. He found her sitting at the piano that his grandfather had passed onto him. Her fingers slid over the keys as though to ghost overtop them, but never actually pressing down to make music.

She didn't need him to make a sound to know he was in the room. She started speaking without a word from him.

"I can't seem to play," she whispered. "I sit at my piano, and I stare at the ivory. I hear these notes in my head, and I see them flying past like I always do. That's how I compose, but then I sit down to play ... and nothing comes out."

Naz fought the urge to frown as he came to lean against the piano. "Why?"

"At first, I wanted to blame *you*. I thought because I was so distracted with you that my desire to make music was just ... gone for a bit. But that was an excuse, and not a reason."

Naz leaned over to let his fingers drift over the keys. He played a simple tune that only took three of his fingers, and a couple of keys. Nothing too serious. He wasn't very fucking good at this anyway.

"So, what's the reason, Roz?"

She glanced up at him, wild-eyed and *scared*. He thought she looked scared. He didn't like that at all.

"I have a deadline coming up. The piece had to be original. *Amazing*. It's a once in a lifetime shot, and the longer I took to feel right about this piece, the worse I felt about it. The more I changed. It wasn't good enough, and because it came from me—"

"You weren't good enough," he murmured.

Roz shrugged, but stayed quiet.

"Roz, you have to know—"

"I'm my own worst critic, and you can tell me I'm the most amazing thing you've ever heard, but that's not going to change what goes on inside my head. It doesn't change what I tell myself."

Naz straightened to his full height, hearing what she said and understanding that better than she knew. Maybe it was because he'd watched his mother go through her own battles throughout his life with things like anxiety and depression. But he got it even if she thought he didn't.

"So, then we start by *rewiring*," he said, coming to sit beside her on the bench. "For every negative thing we hear inside our minds, we tell ourselves five positive things. You hear, *I'm so terrible*. And so you say, *No one else sounds like I do; no one else creates what I do; I am talented; I am worthy; and I can do this*. That's what you do. We can start now."

Roz glanced over at him, and laughed. "Naz—"

"I can do it for you, if you want. You tell me the bad things, I repeat the good things."

She shook her head. "You're crazy."

Not at all.

"I'll do it but on *one* condition."

Roz grinned. "What's that?"

"For every time we have to do this—you say something bad, and I return something good—then you have to play that piece you composed for the audition in Australia." At her curious glance his way, he shrugged. "Your brother mentioned it to me a while back, but when you didn't say anything about it, I figured you didn't want to talk about it. I take it that's the once in a lifetime thing, right?"

Roz sighed. "I'm going to fuck up so bad."

"You're going to nail it. You're going to have the whole fucking crowd on their feet. You're going to be beautiful. You will be amazing. You *are* amazing, Roz."

It took her a second, and then two.

He'd done what he said.

She said something bad.

He came back with five good things.

"I can do this all night," he murmured, "but you know the deal. Your turn, baby."

Her hands found the keys again, and music came out. Hesitant, he thought. He heard the missteps she made, but he thought that might have just been nerves because he was sitting so close to her, and didn't she usually do this sort of thing on her own?

"That was horrible," Roz mumbled when she finished.

"Better than what I can do," he countered. "And it came out of your head, no one else's. You did that. You *created* something. That talent is *yours*. You own this, Roz."

"You don't have to—"

"Yes, I do. Play. That's the deal."

Roz's fingers hit the keys again, but this time, she looked at him while she played. "I love you, Naz."

Naz grinned. "Good fucking thing, huh?"

"Can I do this?"

"If not you, then who?"

# TWENTY-ONE

"Oh, my God, Naz," Roz gasped. "You're not even supposed to be in here!"

She felt his chuckled whisper along her skin as his hands curved around her ass to grab tight to her hips. He'd already pushed the chiffon of her skirt high to get better access, and dragged her lace panties down to her fucking knees. Bent over the bed of her hotel room with her legs wide, and this man behind her … it was breaking every single rule today.

No sex.

No distractions.

Nothing to put her off her game.

And here was fucking Nazio Donati to do exactly that and *more*. But fuck both of them because she loved him for doing this; sneaking into her hotel room, and teasing her just long enough to get up her skirt when she only had two hours to go before audition time.

"Bet you were fucking going crazy in here," he murmured against the shell of her ear. His words were punctuated with one hard thrust of his hips that filled her full of his cock, and sent her flying up to her tiptoes at the same time. The sound that fell from her lips was high, and broken. The relief that swam through her bloodstream was unlike anything she'd ever felt before. "Bet you were overthinking, and worrying too goddamn much, weren't you?"

She was.

Way too much.

And now all she could think about was the fact she'd really like him to fuck her harder, and make her forget about everything. Only he could do that for her, but especially like this.

Roz only got the chance to suck in one good breath before Naz took all her air away when he started slamming into her from behind. The hard wood of the sleigh bed bit into her thighs, but all she felt was bliss. His mouth was still on the shell of her ear, whispering and promising and taking away all of that self-doubt that she'd tried to hide for so long.

How could she be unworthy when she was amazing?

That's what he told her.

97

But as quickly as she heard those words, she was lost in sensation, too. Of him fucking her, and how his fingers felt digging into her hips to yank her harder against him. A raw, fast beat that felt a little too wild but was perfect just the same.

God.

She'd needed this.

Needed him.

It was only when his teeth found the pulse point at her throat, and nipped that she finally tumbled over that edge. For a moment, it felt like time was suspended. Roz was just hanging on by the very tips of her fingers. Noise, and sound, and life … what was any of that when she felt like *this*?

"Oh, my God," she breathed.

"Fuck, fuck, *fuck*," Naz muttered thickly against her throat. One last, hard thrust accompanied his words before she felt him jerk inside her. Emptying into latex, and his hands shaking against her hips. "Yeah, shit, I needed that, too."

Roz found herself laughing as breathless as it was. "*Why?*"

"Because I'm fucking nervous, too."

Was he?

Her nerves were just … well, gone.

Now.

"But that doesn't matter," she heard him whisper along the column of her throat. "You remember that up there, yeah? Just be amazing, Roz, because that's what you are. I'll be right there waiting when you're done."

That was best part, she knew. It didn't matter if she blew this audition. It didn't matter if she fucking nailed it. Because at the end, and tomorrow, or the next day … Naz was still going to be there. Her *family* would still be there. And there would be more auditions, and other companies.

Roz was just getting started.

"Happy birthday, Roz," Naz murmured, kissing the shell of her ear.

She smiled.

Another rule broken for today.

It was supposed to be *just* the audition day, not her birthday. They were supposed to celebrate all that tomorrow. Turning eighteen, and all the rest. Kyle's demands to keep Roz on point, and in total focus for this audition.

Naz was damned determined to break all of those rules.

Roz didn't even mind.

"You better get the hell out of here before Kyle comes and finds you," she mumbled against the bed. "He'll be in a fit, and then I'll have to listen to him the whole way to the audition."

Because yep, Naz wasn't even allowed to drive Roz anywhere. She had to focus on the day, and the audition, and nothing else. Kyle's demands, despite how loudly and often she had protested about it.

Naz made a noise that sounded a lot like annoyance. "Yeah, I kind of hate that guy."

Roz laughed. "Me, too."

But what could she do?

Nail the audition, she supposed.

She did exactly that, too.

Nailed the audition.

But even after the last note echoed from the piano, and her fingers lifted from the keys, Roz stared at the instrument in front of her like it was the first time she had ever seen it before in her life. She felt the bright lights above the stage bearing down on her, and the way her dress tightened around her body with every quick breath she took. She heard the sounds of feet shuffling and rushing to stand in the crowd as people stood, and then the noise of their applause when they began clapping.

Yet, all she saw was the shiny top of a Baby Grand and the ivory keys barely kissing her fingertips.

Because *she did it*.

Her fingers trembled, but she didn't know why. Her mind shouted for her to stand, and face the crowd as was customary. To bow, and smile gracefully like she had been taught her whole life.

And still, she stared at the piano.

Still, she felt those notes echoing in her mind. A reverberation of the song she had created that slowed from her mind to her fingers and through the piano like an extension of her very person.

Maybe …

Maybe a part of her still thought she wouldn't be able to do it. That she'd freeze, or miss a key. That she would screw up that last stanza when the notes reached an impossibly high, fast rhythm that she had only been able to complete once before.

*With Naz.*

*Stand, stand, stand,* her mind shouted.

Roz did just that, although how gracefully, she wasn't sure. Sweeping her hand along her skirt to move it off the bench, she did a quick bow. She couldn't really see the people in the crowd or the ones who were meant to score and judge her performance because of the lights. But she was grateful for that, too.

Somehow, she remembered to smile.

Somehow, she remembered to breathe.

Above her head, Roz saw a red light flick on and off three times. A signal for the performer on stage to move along for the next person. The lights were still too bright. The crowd was still impossibly loud.

She gave a little wave as she headed for the exit on the right side of the stage.

There he was.

Already waiting.

Roz's steps turned into a run because Naz was really the only person she wanted in that moment. Oh, sure, she wanted her parents. She wanted to hear her mentor tell her what she already knew—this fucking audition was all hers.

But right then, she just wanted *him*.

Naz caught Roz in his embrace when she launched herself at him. Those strong arms of his wrapped around her like a cage that was never going to let her go. God, she didn't want him to.

She hadn't realized it until one of his hands wiped at her cheek, but tears had make tracks down her face. But they were good tears; *happy* tears.

Roz didn't know what she expected Naz to say in those seconds. Congratulations, maybe. Or even a confirmation of how amazing he kept telling her she was.

He surprised her.

He was always doing that.

With his lips pressed against hers, he murmured, "I can't believe you're mine, Rosalynn Puzza."

# TWENTY-TWO

Naz stuffed his hands in his pockets, and eyed the familiar house in front of him. Never once had he felt out of place or nervous coming here. He could walk up those steps like he'd done from the time he learned how to fucking walk, and stroll right through the front door as if *he* actually lived here. Even though he didn't and never had.

It never mattered. Those doors had always been opened for him no matter what. He could come and go as he pleased. Park his four-wheeler in the garage as a kid, and join them at the table for supper with no questions asked. Drank too much as a teenager, and didn't want to go home? He could come *here*.

Next to his own home, this place was his safe haven.

So why did he feel so fucking nervous right now? Why was he looking at Zeke and Katya's home like he'd never been past the threshold of the front door? *Why* were his goddamn hands sweaty?

This wasn't like Naz at all.

"You going to stand out there in the driveway all afternoon, or what?" he heard a familiar voice call.

Naz found his godfather standing on the top of the steps. Zeke leaned against the railing with an easy posture, and a similarly welcoming smile. All of that meant good things because that was the thing about Zeke. He wasn't very good at hiding when he was pissed off at someone, or rather, he couldn't be bothered to try and hide it.

"I was thinking, actually," Naz admitted.

"About what, exactly?"

"How many times I've been here before, I guess. All the shit Luca and I used to do when we were kids. You know, all of that."

Zeke hummed under his breath. "A whole lifetime of memories for you two, I suppose."

"So far."

"You've got lots left to go. That's what Cross and I wanted, you know? The same thing we had as kids growing up. Someone to watch our back because we knew nobody else was going to. We could always count on each other in that way."

Naz nodded. "Yeah, I know."

Zeke cleared his throat, and straightened to his full height. "So, are you coming in, or are you going to keep standing there like an idiot all morning?"

"Thanks for that."

"You're welcome, *principe.*"

Zeke said nothing else, but rather, turned on his heels and headed inside the house. He left the door open. A silent offer for Naz to follow if he wanted. He did exactly that, and took the time to remove his shoes and coat inside the house. Eventually, he found Zeke in the man's office where he was digging through a drawer.

"Roz isn't here," Zeke said. "She's out shopping with her mother. Apparently, she needs to ship *all the things* to Australia within the week, or they're not going to get there in time for her to have them when she gets there."

At the mention of Australia, Naz wanted to both smile and frown. Funny how that worked. He was fucking ecstatic that Roz had nailed the audition. And not to mention, within a week, she got the call. The official, *we would love to invite you to our company.* Her spot was to be filled in a month and a half. A month after his sister's wedding.

They hadn't really got in to the details of what day she was going to officially get on a plane, but Naz knew that conversation was coming. He didn't want to see her go. Fuck him straight to hell because he just wanted to keep her here.

At the same time, this was her dream. This was what she was made to do; what she *wanted* to do. There was no way in hell he was going to hold her back from doing all her amazing things.

So, yeah.

He was going to keep being sad and happy.

Privately sad.

Happy to everyone else.

"I know she isn't here," Naz said, taking a seat when Zeke gestured at the chair across from his desk. Once seated, he pulled out the glasses he had to wear when he read or used the computer just to have something in his hands to focus on. His nerves were fucking ridiculous today. "That's why I came over today."

Zeke glanced at his watch, saying, "Strange time for you to be around. Usually, you're in the middle of the city working."

Naz shrugged. "Nobody's calling to send me running like a fucking *cafone* all over the city. I'm not going to speak on it lest my fucking luck run out, huh?"

His godfather laughed. "Sure, sure."

"Plus, I might have mentioned to Dad that I needed a minute or two today to do something important."

Zeke straightened in his chair, and folded his arms over his chest as he eyed Naz from across the desk. "Something to do with me, yeah?"

"He probably called you right after I hung up."

"Probably," Zeke agreed. "You know how your father is. He's a fucking gossip, but only with me." Then, Zeke turned serious when he muttered, "Never tell him I told you that because he'll try to bust my mouth, and we're too old for that shit. And I *really* don't want to hear Catherine and Katya bitching about it all. Got it?"

Naz chuckled. "Got it."

But where was the lie?

"You're not going to ask her to stay in New York, are you?" Zeke asked quietly when Naz let the silence stretch on between them. "Rosalynn, I mean."

"I don't need you to tell me who you mean. I know."

"Well, are you?"

Naz glanced up from the glasses in his hands, and shook his head. "Nah, I'm not. I *want* to, you know? We're just getting started, her and I. The last thing I want is for her to be on the other side of the world for God knows how long. I'm never leaving New York for a good spread of time— we both know it. So, yeah, I want to."

"But you won't."

"She needs to do her amazing things. And some of those things won't always include me," Naz murmured.

"Far beyond your age, *principe*."

"Something like that." Naz sighed, and glanced up at the ceiling. "We'll figure it out. Vacations to different spots. I'll fly her way when I'm on a run, or something. She'll come back here for holidays …. *maybe*."

"There'll be time."

But how long would they have to do that? It was a question that plagued Naz. And at the same time, he figured, what did it matter?

If it was one year, five years, or a fucking decade … what did it matter? He wasn't going anywhere. He was still going to be standing in the same spot waiting for her to come back his way.

That's how this *love thing* worked, apparently.

"And you've still got a little while before you need to worry about any of that," Zeke said. "A whole month and a half, right?"

"Yeah, speaking of which …"

Zeke smiled. "Mmm, the whole reason you're here."

Naz chuckled, and rolled his eyes. "You know, if Dad is just going to tell you everything … then why make me go through the semantics of actually *asking*? Seems like a waste of time."

"Or I like watching you squirm, Nazio."

Yeah, or that.

Naz sighed. "I thought Roz might like to go to Cece's wedding with me. *But* I also know it's going to a publicized event, and for a long time, you've kept her out of that. She's barely been photographed at all. Certainly not on the arm of a Cosa Nostra soldier at the wedding of a boss's daughter."

"Circumstance because she was always away at school, not because I was attempting to hide her away from this life, actually. She knows what I am, and what I do. I never hid it from my children, Nazio. A lot like your mother and father. When it comes *your* time, I suggest you do the same."

*Huh.*

"But," Zeke said, "you can still ask. Because I'm enjoying this."

Of course, he was.

"Would you allow me to take Roz to Cece's wedding, Zeke?"

"You're a little late in asking me to take her out, aren't you?"

Naz scratched at the bit of facial hair growing on his jaw. Soon, his father was going to bark at him to shave it because made men couldn't have facial hair, and he wasn't a special fucking snowflake just because he wasn't made yet. So was his life.

"So, maybe I did this a little bit backward."

Zeke chuckled dryly. "A little?"

"Give me something."

"Never, *principe*. Nothing is coming easy to you."

"Yeah, make me work for it."

"Exactly that," Zeke countered.

"I shouldn't have been a shit, then. Came to you first, and talked. Whatever."

Zeke waved a hand. "Eh, I don't give a shit, really."

Naz's head snapped up, and he found Zeke was grinning in that way of his. Like he was *greatly* enjoying this moment and nothing more.

"You're just like your father, Nazio. You realize that, don't you?"

Naz tugged on the beanie on his head. "Maybe too much, yeah."

Zeke laughed. "Nah, just enough, Naz. Just fucking enough."

# TWENTY-THREE

"Okay, let's bring down a few wisps of hair, a bit more hairspray, and I think we're done," the stylist said as she moved around Roz to grab a fine-tooth comb. "You were right—up was better than down."

Roz simply smiled at the woman, but inside, she was thinking *duh*. She knew what looks worked best with her. She'd been doing her own hair for concerts all these years. Up was *always* better. Especially when someone was going to be moving a lot. Like tonight.

A wedding meant dancing.

"Oh, good, you're almost done. We're running late this morning."

Roz found her mother in the bathroom doorway. The stylist Katya had hired to come in and do all the ladies' hair and makeup was part of the reason they were late. She seemed to want to argue with both Katya and Roz about what they wanted done for their looks instead of just doing what they asked. It was kind of annoying because had she just done her own hair and makeup like she wanted, then they would have been done already and dressed. But *no*, her mother wanted this day to be no stress.

So much for that.

She suspected her mother wouldn't hire the woman again.

"Just about, yep," the woman chirped.

Katya gave Roz a smile. "Great—come find me after. I have your dress laid out."

"Is Naz here yet?"

"Not yet."

*Damn.*

Roz's fingers itched to find her phone, and shoot off a text to Naz just to find out where he was. It was hard to say if he would even answer, though. It was his sister's wedding, after all. He was one of the groomsmen, so she suspected he had a whole host of things to take care of before she was even going to see him. Pictures, and the whole works.

"So," the stylist drawled after Katya left," I hear you're going to be some big pianist in Australia, huh?"

Roz glanced up at the woman.

*Big pianist* was a little offensive. She'd nailed an audition against fifteen other pianists that came from all around the world to compete for one single spot in a well-known, world-class company. She'd worked her whole life for a single moment in time that was over before she'd even realized it, and now her whole life was about to change again.

In good ways, sure, but still.

It was a change.

Roz simply settled on saying, "Yeah, I guess so."

Thankfully, the stylist didn't bother to make much more chitchat after that. Roz was grateful. She had way too many other things on her mind. About today, and beyond. She couldn't quite put her finger on what was making her so damned nervous at the moment, but it was there and it wouldn't let up.

Australia was just one of those things.

One of many things.

Roz just wanted to focus on today. She was going to do that, no matter what. She figured it would be a lot easier to do once Naz was at her side.

But until then ... she was just going to have to deal with those butterflies in her stomach. Even if she didn't know why she was feeling them to begin with.

"*Perfect*," her mother murmured, appraising the dress Roz wore once all the many little buttons had been done up on the back. Despite the fact she wasn't actually in the wedding, her soft peach gown with a delicate chiffon skirt and an off-the-shoulder top matched the color scheme of the wedding. "You and Naz will match then, hmm?"

Roz smoothed her hands down the front of the dress. "I haven't seen him yet. I haven't bothered to send him a message either. He's probably busy. I'll see him later once we're at the church, and everything."

Katya smiled, but said nothing about Naz. Instead, she said, "Today is a big day for you, yes?"

"Why would you think that?"

"Why wouldn't I, Roz?"

She gave her mother a look in the mirror, but Katya was too busy clasping a necklace around Roz's throat. A chunky piece that made a statement, and glittered under the lights. All things she loved about jewelry, really.

"You're saying that you aren't even a little bit nervous about today?"

Roz pressed her lips together to keep from grinning. Maybe her mother knew her a little too well for her own good. "And if I was?"

"Maybe talking about it will help."

"It's not even *my* wedding."

"No, but it is an important wedding for people like us. And you know what I mean about *that*. Men like your father, and Naz's father. *Nazio*, too, I imagine. It's always a big day when a *principessa* marries. Everyone and anyone shows up for it. This guest list is what, four-hundred people deep, and that was before we get into the plus ones."

Oh, God.

Roz couldn't even hide the way her heart raced at that statement.

"Mmhmm," her mother said as though she could read her daughter's mind. "Talk to me, Roz."

"A lot of people, I guess."

"You are going to play a piece at the reception, too, aren't you?"

"That doesn't bother me."

"No, being with him like this does, yes?"

Yeah.

Katya knew her far too well.

"It's not like the important people don't already know about me and Naz," Roz said. "I guess I just never really took in to account what it would mean when the rest of the world knew, too."

Because that was what today would mean. She was stepping out on the arm of Nazio Donati. *Genius.* Son of a Cosa Nostra boss. Grandson of *two* bosses. A mother and grandmother who were as dangerous as they were pretty. His legacy and name ran far deeper than hers ever could.

Roz was not stupid.

She was not innocent.

She didn't talk about the life because it never mattered to her. But she wasn't stuck with her head in the sand. She knew exactly where Naz came from, and what it meant for their kind of people to step out together like they were going to do today.

Expectations came with it.

People *talked*.

Roz hadn't really thought about any of that until today. It'd never really occurred to her that, in a way, she was going to be in a spotlight she'd never faced before. Even if this wasn't her fucking wedding.

That was a little overwhelming.

"There's going to be reporters," her mother murmured, fixing a stray strand of Roz's hair. "And you will be in socialite magazines tomorrow. They will speculate, and say things. None of it will matter. You will meet face after face that you may never meet again in your lifetime tonight, but simply smile and be gracious as you are. It's just as much about showing you off as it is making a statement."

Roz blinked. "Is it?"

"What?"

"Making a statement and showing me off."

Her mother laughed, and leaned in to kiss her daughter's cheek as her hands squeezed Roz's shoulders supportively. "I'm quite sure he's going to enjoy doing it, too. Why wouldn't he?"

"Roz!"

Her brother's shout echoed from somewhere downstairs.

"What, Luca?"

"Naz is here. Car's warm. Stop playing in the mirror. You look fine."

Roz smiled.

Apparently, she wasn't going to have to wait to see Naz at all. He'd made time. It made her feel better in a way. About a lot of different things.

She was going to need him to keep making time.

Beyond today …

She needed him.

# TWENTY-FOUR

"Roz, come help!"

"Nazio, get over here!"

Naz cursed under his breath as he had to go one way, and Roz was pulled in an entirely different direction in the back halls of the church. The last sight he caught of her was the apologetic smile and small shrug she gave him at the end of the hallway before she was pulled into a room, and gone from his view altogether.

*Shit.*

"Oh, stop looking so sour," Catherine told her son, dragging Naz's attention away from where Roz had disappeared to. "You've been with her all morning, Naz. I am *sure* you can go ten minutes without her."

"Doubtful," Naz muttered under his breath.

Oh, he certainly could be forced away from Roz. It was a whole other matter on whether or not he actually wanted to be taken away from her. Because he didn't. *At all.* He wanted and needed to get as much fucking time with her as he could because all too soon, she was going to be half way across the goddamn world.

But today wasn't the day for that. It wasn't the day for him to get in to all of that shit because it was a happy day. Not *his* happy day even if he was happy. But a happy day nonetheless.

His sister's wedding.

Cross shot his son a look from the side—a silent *shut up, Nazio*—as he worked on fixing a little boy's tie—one of his man's sons. "There you are, Junior. Go find your Papa, huh?"

"Thank you, sir."

His father patted the boy on the top of the head before the kid darted off to find his father. Standing straight, Cross gave Nazio a one-over, and nodded.

"At least I no longer have to fix your ties," his father said.

"That's debatable," his mother countered. "Naz, why is your knot—"

Naz rolled his eyes upward, and zoned his mother out as she started fussing over his fucking tie that was perfectly fine. There was nothing wrong with the knot, and by the time she was done with it, the damn thing would look exactly the same as it had before she got her hands on it. But that was his mother, and there wasn't very much he could do about her need to fuss when she was stressed out. So, instead of telling her to leave him be, he let her fuck around with his tie for a good couple of minutes before his father decided to step in and save the day.

He heard his father's chuckle. "Oh, leave him be, Catty."

"But—"

"Let him go in and see Cece for a minute before we all have to get going and everyone starts rushing. She's got five minutes, doesn't she?"

Catherine passed her husband a look. "Fine. *You're* not ready."

His father was already heading down the hallway, ticking a finger over his shoulder as he went. "On my way there now."

"*Late.*"

"The boss is never late, Catherine. Everyone else is always *early.*"

"He is when his wife says so!"

Naz couldn't help but smirk at the way his mother fake-glared at her husband's back. No doubt, his father knew it, too.

"Well," Naz said, fixing the jacket of his tux, "if you're just about done with your foreplay, I'd like to go talk to my sister before I walk Roz to her seat."

His mother's eyes widened, and her gaze turned on him. "That was not fore—"

"Mmhmm. Laundry room, Ma."

Every single time his parents got in one of their moods, he was thrust back into the memory of coming home way too early and kind of finding his parents in a compromising position in the laundry room. He hadn't gone far enough to actually *see* them, but with the way his fucking brain worked … he didn't need to see to know. Or to create a goddamn image that was forever burned into his brain.

Stupid, genius brain.

Her cheeks pinked. "*Nazio!*"

"Never gonna forgive you for that," he muttered. "*Ever.*"

"Oh, my God," his mother huffed, "go see your sister."

"That was the plan, yep."

Naz barely dodged the playful slap his mother aimed at the back of his head before he slipped inside his sister's dressing room. It seemed like, for the moment, it was only Cece and her makeup artist in the room. He doubted his sister was getting very much quiet time today. He'd already made the trip across the church to see—and possibly threaten—her husband-to-be, but this was the first time he actually got to see his sister today.

"Hey, you look great, Naz," Cece said, finally noticing him. She gave him a smile, but quickly went back to doing what the makeup artist told her. "Where's Ma?"

"Pestering Dad. And aren't I supposed to be the one telling you how beautiful you look today? It's *your* day, Cece."

His sister—who looked entirely too much like their mother, but with a mind like their father—grinned over at him. "I know how I look, thank you."

Yeah, just like their mom and dad.

For a moment, the two siblings stared at one another. Naz thought, in those seconds, their entire childhood passed before his eyes. Compliments of that brain of his, there wasn't one moment of his life growing up with Cece as his big sister that he couldn't remember.

She taught him how to walk.

He took his first steps for her.

It was going to be some kind of fucked up situation for him when he woke up next week, and realized his sister wasn't in the same city as him. Sure, they didn't hang out or talk as much as they used to ... life kept them busy like that ... but damn, she was always there. A drive or phone call away when he needed her.

*Always.*

Cece smiled a bit, as though she could read his mind. "California isn't that far away, Naz."

"Yeah, I keep trying to tell myself that about Australia, too ... but fuck it if I don't still feel like shit over it, huh? Except I know I shouldn't feel like that about it at all. Same with this. It's good—you going to Cali with Juan, that's *good*. And I still feel like ... well, fuck what I feel. It's about you, right? You're happy."

His sister didn't need for him to explain. She already knew.

He told Cece everything.

"You'll figure out a way to make it work, Naz," Cece said. "You're too brilliant not to."

Naz slipped down *another* back hallway in the church in search of Roz. Someone had said they thought they had seen her come this way, and he felt like he was on a wild fucking goose chase because—

"Jesus Christ!"

He almost fell face first into the floor of an unknown room when Roz suddenly appeared in the doorway, and yanked him inside. It took him far too long to realize it wasn't just *any* unknown room.

No, it was the goddamn confessional.

111

But it was way too late to think about that because she had shut the door, and backed him up against it with a kiss that silenced his chaotic mind. He couldn't even ask what in the hell she was doing because her hands were already undoing his pants, and slipping beneath his boxer-briefs. Add the tightening of her palm around his hard dick, and the fast strokes of her hand that woke him up in an instant, and Naz was a goner.

He was already trying to get his hands under the many layers of chiffon keeping her hidden from him.

"Why do these dresses have so many fucking layers?" he growled against her mouth.

"Because I don't think *this* is what you're supposed to be doing when you wear them, Naz."

Her laughter quickly melted into the sweetest moan when he yanked her across the room, and she fell into his lap as he found a chair that was *not* meant for this. He knew the chair wasn't meant for fucking because he'd sat on it at least once a year from the time he turned thirteen to confess his sins to his priest.

*Yeah.*

"This is *not* going in my next confession," he said in a long groan as Roz fit him between her thighs, and then lowered down fast. Too fast, maybe. It took the fucking air right out of his lungs, and all he could do was grab onto her hips for some kind of stability. "No damn way."

Her laughter was there again. Filling up the room, and his mind, and his soul. He was probably going to miss hearing that the most when she was gone.

*Breathless.*

So sweet.

It only lasted long enough for him to pull her in for another kiss, and then she was riding him the way he liked. Fast, and wild. Fingernails digging into his shoulders, and her tongue warring with his. He got to swallow every one of her pretty little sounds while she took what she wanted, and fucked them both to oblivion.

What a fucking way to spend a wedding.

Naz didn't linger on those thoughts for long because something else was taking up space in his mind. Like the way Roz was shaking, how her hands tightened on him, and how her sounds came out a little higher.

His balls tightened, and heat shot up his spine.

*Fuck.*

The second she came, he was right there, too.

"*Holy Christ,*" he mumbled into Roz's neck.

Yeah, there was definitely a special place in hell with his name stamped on the door for this. Naz was going there with a smile on his face. He didn't even care.

112

Then, he had another thought.

"No fucking condom, Roz," he muttered.

He felt her small shrug. "It's okay. I have the shot done."

"*Still.*"

Mistakes happened.

He didn't think a baby would be good for either of them right now, but especially not her. It wasn't like having a little one would do anything but hold her back when she was trying to rise higher. He never wanted to hold her back. Not in that way, or any other way.

Roz straightened on his lap, and her fingertips ghosted over his face with a soft touch. "Sometimes, I want to stay right here with you."

Naz smiled. "And sometimes you wanna go, right?"

"Yeah."

"You're going to go," he told her, "and you're going to be amazing. You're going to do the thing you want to do more than anything because I don't ever want you to wonder what might have been if you didn't take the chance."

"But what about—"

"We'll figure it out. Because it's just a moment in time. That's all it's going to be. And then there'll be another moment. A different one. There'll be a moment just like this one today, except you'll be wearing a white dress, and I'll be at the other end waiting for you. But in between, we'll just have to figure it out, okay?"

Roz nodded. "Yeah, okay."

"I love you, Roz."

"With my whole heart, Naz."

He was about to drag her in for another kiss, but a knock on the door stopped him. And a *voice* …

"If you two are just about fucking done in there," Luca grumbled, "people are *waiting*."

Well, shit.

Naz figured … story of his life. He just had a whole new chapter now with Roz. And they were just getting started.

# EPILOGUE

*Three months later …*

"So, Australia is treating you well, then?"

Roz laughed at the way her brother grinned on the other end of the video chat. "You could say that."

"You have survived this long, I guess."

"*Barely.*" Roz shuddered. "A spider got into my apartment last week, and it was the size of a saucer, Luca. When I say the sound that came out of me was not human, I *mean it.*"

Her brother didn't even try to hide his laughter. She just rolled her eyes because of course, it was funny to him. He was in New York where for a good portion of the year, the air hurt his face when he went outside. There was no chance of gigantic spiders living *there*.

The bastard.

"Who killed it for you?"

"Neighbor came in and got it out. Didn't kill it. Put it outside."

Luca looked horrified. "But what if it gets back in?"

"That's what I fucking said!"

And all her neighbor had done was gave her a look that silently said *foreigner*. Not that she could blame the guy, really.

"Really, I like it here," Roz said, "and everybody's nice. I just miss home sometimes, and I *really* miss home when it's quiet, I guess."

Luca nodded. "Yeah, I bet."

But she was living her dream.

Doing her *thing*.

Roz couldn't complain about that. Not at all.

"I hear you're headlining at the Concert Hall next week," Luca said. "Every night, too."

Yeah, she was.

Her name was in fucking lights. The concert piano was shined, and tuned every single day. She had a different gown for every fifteen minutes.

It was amazing.

But all she could think about was the fact Naz was going to be there. It would be the first time she saw him since moving to Australia, and she couldn't wait. He was coming to see her first headlining act because he didn't want to just hear about it. No, he wanted to actually *see it.*

So yeah, her focus wasn't anywhere near what was coming up. It was firmly stuck on the man that was about to make his way across the world just to be with her for a couple of short days.

"It's going to be good," Roz said.

"I need pictures."

"You'll all get them."

"And videos." Luca grinned. "My baby sister headlining something like that? I need proof, and it gives me bragging rights."

"You're such a shit, Luca."

"I know." Her brother's gaze shifted from view when a buzzing sounded on the other end of the video call. She thought it might be his phone. "So, hey … early gift from me to you as a congrats for this whole headlining thing, huh?"

Roz's brow furrowed. "What?"

"I got you an early gift. Promised to handle a bunch of crap, and make sure nobody would even notice he was gone for a few weeks. You can thank me later. Go open your door, Roz."

Her brother winked before reaching forward, and closing his laptop, effectively ending their video call. Without even a proper goodbye. Roz might have been confused if she wasn't so freaking annoyed, but it was the knock that echoed throughout her quiet apartment that took her attention away for the moment.

She didn't even get the chance to get up from her seat before whoever it was knocked again.

It was way too late at night for one of her new friends to be coming over. And her apartment building was full of decent people who also wouldn't be banging on her door this late, too.

She didn't even think to check the peephole. Maybe she should have, though. Maybe it would have prepared her heart for when she found Nazio standing on the other side of the door looking like God's gift to women in dark wash jeans, a white tee, and his leather jacket.

He had his beanie pulled down over his ears, and his glasses on. He rarely wore those unless he was reading something. She thought he must have taken a red-eye, or had a hell of a long layover if his eyes were so tired that he needed his glasses.

But he looked fucking cute wearing them, too.

He looked up.

She smiled.

"Long flight?" she asked.

Naz chuckled. "But worth it."

115

She already had her arms open, and he was there to catch her when she darted forward. Warmth, and strength, and *love*.

"Told you," he said, "we're gonna figure this out, babe."

Yeah, they would.

That was a promise.

# ABOUT THE AUTHOR

Bethany-Kris is a Canadian author, lover of much, and mother to four young sons, one cat, and three dogs. A small town in Eastern Canada where she was born and raised is where she has always called home. With her boys under her feet, a snuggling cat, barking dogs, and a spouse calling over his shoulder, she is nearly always writing something ... when she can find the time.

Find Bethany-Kris at:
www.bethanykris.com
www.bethanykris.blogspot.com
www.facebook.com/bethanykriswrites
www.twitter.com/bethanykris
www.instagram.com/bethany.kris
www.pinterest.com/bethanykris

Sign up to Bethany-Kris's New Release Newsletter here:
http://eepurl.com/bf9lzD.

# OTHER BOOKS

Andino + Haven
Duty
Vow


John + Siena

Loyalty
Disgrace


Cross + Catherine

Always
Revere
Unruly
The Companion
Naz & Roz


Guzzi Duet

Unraveled, Book One
Entangled, Book Two


DeLuca Duet

Waste of Worth: Part One
Worth of Waste: Part Two

Standalone Titles

Effortless
Inflict
Cozen
Captivated
Dishonored

Donati Bloodlines

Thin Lies
Thin Lines
Thin Lives
Behind the Bloodlines
The Complete Trilogy

Filthy Marcellos

Antony
Lucian
Giovanni
Dante
Legacy
A Very Marcello Christmas
The Complete Collection

Seasons of Betrayal

Where the Sun Hides
Where the Snow Falls
Where the Wind Whispers
Seasons: The Complete Seasons of Betrayal Series

Gun Moll Trilogy

Gun Moll
Gangster Moll
Madame Moll

The Chicago War

Deathless & Divided
Reckless & Ruined
Scarless & Sacred
Breathless & Bloodstained
The Complete Series

The Russian Guns

The Arrangement
The Life
The Score
Demyan & Ana
Shattered
The Jersey Vignettes

Find more on Bethany-Kris's website at www.bethanykris.com.

www.ingramcontent.com/pod-product-compliance
Lightning Source LLC
Chambersburg PA
CBHW052006170626
46808CB00007B/2795